"You're On My Side Of The Bed,"

Angus growled.

"I'm freezing," Hillary said groggily.

"I can warm you nicely." With some glee he took her into his arms and kissed her.

She kissed him back drowsily and slid her arms up to him, too. Then she ruined everything. "How kind you are. I needed so badly to be held. I'm so worried about my sister."

Her words threw him. She only wanted support— was that why she was there in his arms? Well, damn.

She then proceeded to go back to sleep!

Men had it tough, Angus thought. They needed to get things back under control!

Dear Reader:

Welcome! You hold in your hand a Silhouette Desire—your ticket to a whole new world of reading pleasure.

A Silhouette Desire is a sensuous, contemporary romance about passions, problems and the ultimate power of love. It is about today's woman—intelligent, successful, giving—but it is also the story of a romance between two people who are strong enough to follow their own individual paths, yet strong enough to compromise, as well.

These books are written by, for and about every woman that you are—wife, mother, sister, lover, daughter, career woman. A Silhouette Desire heroine must face the same challenges, achieve the same successes, in her story as you do in your own life.

The Silhouette reader is not afraid to enjoy herself. She knows when to take things seriously and when to indulge in a fantasy world. With six books a month, Silhouette Desire strives to meet her many moods, but each book is always a compelling love story.

Make a commitment to romance—go wild with Silhouette Desire!

Best,

Isabel Swift
Senior Editor & Editorial Coordinator

LASS SMALL
Goldilocks and the Behr

Silhouette Desire

Published by Silhouette Books New York

America's Publisher of Contemporary Romance

SILHOUETTE BOOKS
300 East 42nd St., New York, N.Y. 10017

ISBN: 0-373-05437-8

First Silhouette Books printing July 1988

Printed in the U.S.A.

Books by Lass Small

Silhouette Romance

An Irritating Man #444
Snow Bird #521

Silhouette Desire

Tangled Web #241
To Meet Again #322
Stolen Day #341
Possibles #356
Intrusive Man #373
To Love Again #397
Blindman's Bluff #413
Goldilocks and the Behr #437

LASS SMALL

writes concerning *Goldilocks and the Behr* that "The six in our house number lost a nail and was hanging in the position of a nine. That teased my imagination— a correct number that had become incorrect. When it came time to continue Tate's story, I needed a reason for Hillary to meet the Behr, and I used that ploy. Then I needed a reason for her to be in Chicago, and gradually the plot evolved. But it all started with a missing nail."

To
The Behrs—Jerry and Bob
and their three cubs

One

Hillary Lambert was a hunter of stolen children, so she had chosen to live in Kansas City, Missouri, in order to be centrally located in this big country. On that hot July evening as she crossed the apartment complex, more than one man's gaze was drawn to her. Hillary was blond, slender, twenty-five and tired.

She paused in the entry of her building to empty her mailbox, and she almost missed the letter as she sorted through all the mail addressed to Occupant. Over the years there must have been a lot of people who'd lived in her apartment who had sent off for catalogs, because the stream of junk mail was endless.

With practiced patience, Hillary jiggled the key in her door lock. It always took a while before the lock worked. She opened the door, still frowning at the envelope. It was a letter from her sister.

Hillary dumped the armload of junk mail into a handy wastebasket as she kicked off her shoes and dropped her purse onto the chair close by. She had a strange feeling about the letter. Her family were phoners, not writers. She bit her lower lip before she took a bracing breath and tore the envelope open.

Each time she read it, the words said the same thing: "If you get this letter, I'm probably being held somewhere. Don't panic. I'm sure I'm not in any danger. But if you haven't heard from me after ten days, get in touch with Carter. Don't call the police, and don't tell the family. Yet. I love you, Boy. Tate."

Boy. That nickname went back a long way, to Tate's Tarzan period. At that time Hillary had been a baby and could only fill the role as Tarzan's found child, Boy. But Carter? Hillary didn't know of any Carter.

Tate was a practical woman. While she had great humor, trickery wasn't in her. As weird as the note seemed, Hillary knew it was serious.

It had been through Tate that Hillary had become trained in locating stolen children. Now it could be Tate herself who needed to be located, or she wouldn't have alerted Hillary in this way.

From the wording of the note, Tate appeared to be pretty sure she would be all right. But she wasn't positive. She was making sure that if ten days passed and she hadn't turned up, someone would know that she was missing. So she'd written the letter. But how could Tate expect Hillary to just sit there for ten days, chewing her fingernails, waiting to find out if this snatch was dangerous or not? How strange.

And Carter. Who was Carter? Without a first and last name, Hillary couldn't call information for Chicago and ask for the number. The only way Hillary could call this Carter was to go to Chicago and find Tate's address book and therefore Carter's phone number. So while Tate hadn't actually asked Hillary to come to her, Tate wanted Hillary in Chicago and hunting at the end of ten days.

With an impulsive rejection of Tate's request to wait, Hillary dialed her sister's number. After the fourth ring, Tate's recorded voice said, "Leave your name and number, and I shall get back to you." Tate said the words as if there were no question but that she would call back.

When the beep came, Hillary blurted, "I'm on my way." Somehow she couldn't bring herself to hang up. She finally put her finger on the bar to disconnect. Then she called the Kansas City airport.

She was told it would be three hours until the next plane to Chicago. However, that booking was filled. There wasn't another flight until early the next morning. She could join those on standby for the next flight, or the agent could arrange a sophisticated roundabout, but it would be "busy" traveling, with hours expended in flight time and waiting time. Hillary was too antsy to wait, so she would drive.

Without further hesitation, she prepared herself to go to Chicago and do her waiting there. She chose a selection from her discreet "hunting clothes" and put them in a case. She emptied the spoilables from the fridge and took out the garbage. Then she stopped by the apartment-complex office and told them she'd be away for a while. The office people were used to her departures and wished her luck in her hunting. With troubled eyes, Hillary stopped, looked back at the two women and said, "Thank you."

She decided to rent a car, because parking in Chicago was a nuisance. She took a cab to the rental agency, selected a car and, after putting her things into it, drove by her bank's automatic teller machine. With all the preparations completed, she drove north to Chicago.

Although she found it unbelievable that Tate could be in trouble, it was even spookier for Hillary to realize that in order for Tate to have written that note, she had to have known ahead of time that she was in danger. No kidnappers were going to stand around while Tate dashed off a message to her sister.

As Hillary drove along, she wondered what in the world Tate had gotten into. How could she have become involved in anything dangerous? She was editor of her newspaper's women's page.

In such a job, how could Tate have stumbled across anything that would make her suspect that someone could snatch her? A jealous cook? A designer? A craftsperson? That was too bizarre. Whatever it was that Tate had discovered, it had to be by happenstance and something that was drastically opposed to Tate's old-fashioned code of ethics. It had to be something important to Tate, or the snatch didn't make sense.

But then neither did most of life make any sense, Hillary knew. In order to survive, one rode the waves and didn't rock the boat. But apparently Tate had rocked *somebody's* boat.

With Hillary's traveling around and searching for stolen children, she had keys to the houses of all the extended Lambert family across the country. Ordinarily she would call ahead, but if she did this time, there would be no one there. Tate was missing. How incredible.

Hillary drove the five hundred miles from Kansas City to Chicago on adrenaline, fast food, and fuel stops. It was almost ten the next morning when, still hyper, she arrived in Chicago on the awesome network of crisscrossed six-lane highways. She drove through, taking the correct cutoffs, until she found a branch of the rental agency where she could leave the car. She then took a cab to the tall, convoluted marina structure on Lake Michigan, north of the Loop, where Tate lived.

Hillary had never been to this particular complex. Tate had lived there only about four months, in apartment six, on the second floor. The first floor held management offices, a spa and meeting rooms. Only new tenants lived on the second floor. Ground-level activities, passersby and vehicles along the Outer Drive made the second floor too noisy. Smarter residents moved upward as soon as there were vacancies.

Hillary went through the entrance doors, to be halted at the desk and asked for identification. She hesitated, biting her tongue, wanting to say, "Where were you when Tate was snatched? You claim to keep your tenants secure?" Such questions couldn't be asked until Hillary had more information. First she would have to talk to Carter.

Once Hillary had identified herself to security, they found her name on Tate's list of people who could be admitted. The woman said, "You can take the elevator or the stairway over there. Number six."

Hillary said thank-you, lifted her bag, ignored the elevator and climbed the stairs. The complex had been constructed so that the apartment entrances opened onto inside-facing curving hallways, since the winter winds across the lake could be bitter.

With the prickle of unease she'd felt since she'd first seen Tate's envelope, Hillary turned at the top of the stairs and found the apartment. The door held a bronze number six, and Hillary inserted the key.

The fact that the key stuck and was just as stubborn as her own lock down in Kansas City touched Hillary's consciousness. How irritatingly droll that two sisters living so far apart both had the same lock problem. She wondered if she would ever be able to share the humor of it with her sister. She felt chilled in the July heat.

It took some struggle, but she was so practiced with her own stubborn lock that Tate's finally moved and the door opened. Hillary went in, dumped her stuff on the nearest chair and stepped out of her shoes, just as she always did. An almost all white short-haired cat came to greet her. A cat? When had Tate acquired a cat? Hillary looked around. The apartment didn't look like any other place where her sister had ever lived.

Of course, Tate had only been there four months, but even in that time there would be some mark of her personality. Where was the stuffed fish Tate had bragged about? That hilarious fish.

On the dining-room table were a personal computer and stacks of pages and books. Not tidy. Hillary picked up several pages and looked at them. The figures and graphs made her frown. She thought that was odd work for an English-lit major. There was no desk, therefore no drawer. Where was the address book?

She went into the bedroom. One side of the bed was rumpled. They'd taken Tate from the bed? She would never have willingly left the bed unmade.

Uneasy, Hillary opened the sliding door to the closet and found clothes that surprised her. A few woman's garments, but there were...a man's. Most of the clothes were his. Tate was living with some man? She'd never mentioned that. Where were the rest of her clothes?

If she was living with a man, why had Tate sent the letter to her sister? Why wasn't this man out beating the bushes and looking for Tate? If she knew him well enough to live with him, where was he? Maybe he *was* out looking. He wasn't there. Obviously it was Tate who'd moved in with him. It was a man's apartment. Was he Carter?

No, he couldn't be. If Tate had asked Hillary to contact her lover, she would have given her his number.

Hillary went into the kitchen and found the cat sitting on the counter. Tate with a cat. Wonders never cease. Hillary ran a hand down the appreciative cat's back and asked, "Where's Tate?" The cat purred.

Where was Tate's coffee maker? There was *instant* coffee on the shelf....

That made Hillary go back, open the front door and verify the number. There was a six. This was Tate's apartment. Hillary searched for an address book and found the man's, which held mostly women's names. That caused Hillary to frown. If he was any kind of decent man, why did he still have an address book with other women's names? But Tate had no book. How was Hillary supposed to find this Carter if there was no address book?

In her concentrated search, Hillary had been look-ing for a specific item: the address book. Now she be-came conscious of the type of clothing in the drawers. His. But the woman's clothing was sparse, and... really... not at *all* like Tate. Hillary held up a red nothing and blinked.

What sort of person was this man with whom Tate was living? He must be very different to have caused such a basic change in her tastes. Was *he* the reason Tate was missing?

Even with a very diligent search, Hillary couldn't find one item with his name or any clue as to his oc-cupation. Could he be in some shady trade? No. No matter how attractive the man could be, Tate would never be tempted to couple her life with such a man.

Whoever he was, he had excellent taste in clothing, and it was expensive. His shoes were cared for and evenly worn. He had a good, even stride. He was an athlete; there were weights to lift. He did something with figures and graphs.

There wasn't a checkbook or a bill or any file to identify the man. But there wasn't anything of Tate's, either, that Hillary could recognize. This was very strange.

Hillary sat down on the arm of a chair in the living room and rubbed her tired face. Since the man dealt in charts and graphs, he probably worked in an office and wouldn't be back until after five. It was almost eleven. There wasn't anything she could do until she could talk to this man with whom Tate was living. She might just as well climb in the other side of that wide bed and go to sleep. She was dead tired.

She showered, put on an old oversize T-shirt and panties, then crawled into the made side of the bed.

That side hadn't been slept on. That meant the man had slept in the bed alone last night. Therefore Tate hadn't been taken from the apartment? He wasn't tidy, but her side was still made up.

Hillary knew she needed to sleep. Her head hurt and her mind was fuzzy, yet her brain refused to give up and let her recoup. She dragged herself from the bed, went into the bath and opened the cabinet above the lavatory. No aspirin. But there was a little bottle that said: For Sleep. It had a childproof cap, and, by scraping her fingerpads and breaking a nail, she opened it. The pills were white and so very small that she guessed they were probably harmless. She took one.

Angus Behr came home—to apartment nine—that night at almost five-thirty. Somewhat disgruntled, he reached out and pushed the door's six up into its proper position as a nine. All it would take was one small nail, and maintenance hadn't fixed it yet.

The heat was wicked. He'd strip and put on trunks, go down and swim a hundred laps, then eat somewhere. He inserted his key as his neighbor Jenny sauntered by in a lingering way, with a great, big grin and a soft hello. He gave her a nod. The key worked smoothly, and he went inside.

As his cat came to greet him, Angus saw that there was a purse on the chair by the door and a pair of women's shoes nearby. Odd. He wasn't expecting anyone. No one had a key. He hadn't given security permission for anyone to be allowed inside. He left the door standing open as he looked around and listened. Who'd gotten in? No one in sight, no sound. Alert, he walked over to look into the kitchen. What woman?

With some caution, he went into the bedroom and looked in. There was someone sleeping in his bed! Out cold. He gave the bath and closets quick checks before he walked closer and studied the woman. A good-looking blonde. He grinned. She was sleeping really hard. What was she doing there? He saw her suitcase lying open on the floor by the chest of drawers. He looked back at her, contemplating the situation, before he went over to stand by her and study her as she lay there. She looked deliciously receptive, sprawled so temptingly in his bed. Any man's fancy. She didn't know what she tempted.

He leaned over and shook her shoulder. It was flaccid under his hand and her head wobbled, but she didn't waken. He leaned closer and smelled her breath. Not drunk. No rings. How had she gotten in? She'd had to pass security. They were really tough here. There was no way for a stranger to get into the building. In that whole building, why had she come to his place? Who was she? How had she gotten in?

Considering all that, he went back into the living room, closed the door and locked it. Then he picked up the purse and looked inside. No gun. A wallet. She was Hillary Lambert of Kansas City. Who the hell was Hillary Lambert? She was five feet six inches in height, twenty-five years old, blond, and blue eyed. She had about two hundred dollars cash. A little more. There were American Express and VISA cards. Her checkbook showed a balance of over a thousand dollars.

He couldn't remember ever having met a Hillary Lambert in all his life; and he was sure that if he had, he would have remembered this one. Even her driver's license picture was gorgeous. If she showed up that good in such a picture, it was proof that she was exceptionally good-looking.

He put the wallet back, went into the kitchen and mixed himself a drink, then returned to sit beside her on the bed. Her body rolled toward him somewhat as his weight shifted her, but she continued sleeping soundly. Her lips were parted just a bit, and he was tempted to lean down and kiss them.

To distract himself he rattled the ice in his glass as he wondered what to do about her. At the sound, her tongue tip touched along her upper lip. He watched fascinated, feeling a sexual stirring in his body. Then he realized she must be thirsty. He returned to the kitchen, put some ice and water into a glass and came back to her.

She hadn't moved. He rattled the ice again and asked, "Are you thirsty, Hillary?"

Her lips parted, her chin raised a bit and her tongue again touched her upper lip. It took a bit of control for him not to lean down and touch her mouth with his own tongue, then kiss her. She was in his bed.

He rattled the ice again, and she swallowed rather painfully. She must really be thirsty. Was she ill? He put his hand on her forehead. His palm was cold from the icy glass, and she smiled just a little. He leaned down and kissed her cheek, but her body temperature appeared to be normal. No fever.

She'd turned her head to take his kiss! She must be dreaming of some man. He felt a twinge of indignation. Then he thought how dumb it was that he'd be indignant that this strange woman should be dreaming of some other man! In spite of the fact that she was in his bed, she couldn't possibly know him.

"Here," he said. "Want some water?"

She struggled against the sleep to obey. She apparently was drugged. She didn't look like a druggie. He shifted, leaned down and scooped his hand slowly under her shoulders before lifting her. Bracing her with his arm and shoulder, he held the glass to her lips. Not quite coordinated, she drank slowly, resting between sips, but she almost finished up the glass. Then she sighed and turned toward him, squirming in a snuggling way, making a contented sound that made him tingle erotically as his body reacted.

In his lifting her, the sheet had fallen from her chest, and he saw that the T-shirt she wore was old and worn. And soft. It molded her breasts very intimately. Independently, his hand set the glass on the bedside table and hovered over her. But he did make it hesitate. She was asleep, and he was old enough to have some control.

Very carefully, and rather proud of himself, he laid her back, slid his arm from under her and meticulously straightened the sheet to cover those enticing rounds.

What was he to do about her? Forgetting his plans to swim and eat out, he went back to the kitchen, searched in the freezer compartment, put his usual two frozen dinners into the microwave and set the timer. He fed the cat, wandered around, looked out the window at the lake's surface and watched the sun set. It was very quiet. He went in and looked down at her. He smiled. It was nice to have her there.

As was usual, Angus ate both dinners, watched the news and worked on some papers, with the cat lying on the table, watching him. But tonight he had an unusual addition to his evening's routine. He checked on the woman in his bed who was Hillary Lambert from Kansas City, Missouri.

At bedtime she still lay as she had, sound asleep. He tried again to rouse her, but although she drank from another glass of water, she slept on. He showered, then, as he opened the cabinet, he saw that the bottle of tiny codeine pills had been moved. The doctor had given Angus those pills last year when he'd almost killed himself bench-pressing too much weight. There'd been three pills left. There were now two. She'd had one. No wonder she slept so hard. Why would any woman who should be halfway intelligent take someone else's medication? How did she know what was in that pill?

After he'd put on pajama bottoms and brushed his teeth, he went back into the bedroom to fetch his pillow to go sleep on the couch. From the door he looked back at the unused expanse of his big bed and thought, hell, she wouldn't waken until the next afternoon. It was his bed. He put the pillow back, crawled in, lay down and turned toward her. "Good night, Hillary."

After a minute, she said a faint "Mmm."

That made him grin. It was rather nice having her over there on the other side of his bed. It beat all hell out of just sharing the bed with the cat. He sighed and settled a little more comfortably, thinking about her. Wondering who she was and why she was there, he remembered that she'd turned to meet his mouth when he'd tested her for a fever.

He gave a quick, sharp look, his body tensing a little. Would she? He rolled up onto his elbows and shifted over to her; then, with calculation, he leaned over her and allowed his breath to touch her cheek. She slept on. He touched his warm lips to her cool cheek and waited. Slowly, slowly, she turned her head and, with difficulty, pursed her lips. He kissed her. She didn't draw back. His breath quickened. He lifted his head and saw that she smiled briefly before she sank back into deeper sleep.

Reluctantly he moved back to his side and lay with his hands behind his head as he frowned at the ceiling. The cat jumped up and made itself comfortable between them. It licked and licked and licked. Listening to the cat working away with its tongue, Angus figured being almost all white must make cleaning fur a real pain. Finally the cat curled down and purred. By then Angus had come to the firm agreement that possession was nine-tenths of the law.

What if she never wakened? What if she had a sleeping sickness and she never woke up? He'd keep her. He grinned over at the sleeping woman who shared his bed. It might be very nice and uncomplicated to have a silent, available woman handy in his bed. Especially such a beautiful, well-formed blonde. Yes, it would.

Tomorrow he would call in to his office so that he could stay home and find out about this lovely puzzle. She would have to wake up sometime. After a while he turned out the light and went to sleep.

He woke up hotter than a two-dollar pistol. His arms wound closer around her, and his breath was scorching. He laughed. Pulling her arching into him, he curled to meet her. Pat? Pat, his longtime friend and occasional love? Why would she be back? He groped and whispered, and his hands knew first. Even in those few times, Pat had never worn anything in his bed. Then he remembered Hillary Lambert.

Gradually he released her, and as she murmured a soft protesting sound, it pleased him that being released made her restless. Served her right. What was she doing on his side of the bed? She had no business there. Any strange woman ought to know to stay on her own side of the bed. It was just exactly as it was on a highway: cross the center line and get wrecked.

He got up, went to the bathroom, got a drink of water and paced around the apartment. He went through her purse, hoping there'd be some cigarettes down in the bottom of the thing—but no such luck. He hadn't prowled for a cigarette in two years! She was ruining him! When she woke up she'd better have a hell of a good story to explain her being in his bed.

He sat on the couch, then lay down, then thought, why should *he* be the one to sleep on the damned couch? He stomped back to bed, took more than his share of the sheet and flopped around for some time— deliberately—and pounded his pillow rather harshly. But she didn't move again, and he finally went back to sleep.

When he next wakened, it was light outside, and she was on her stomach in a normal sleep. She moved and yawned, but she slept on. She must have been exhausted when she took that pill. He wondered if she'd driven up from Kansas City the day before. Flown in? Train? Maybe she was on her way *back* to Kansas City.

How had she landed in his lap? Out of all the other people in Chicago, there she was...with him. Why him?

He eased his way out of bed. No sense in startling her. He didn't like hysterical women. Or ones who might be indignant about a man who just wanted to sleep in his own bed. He tidied his side so that it didn't look as if he'd shared it with her. Then he took his underwear out of his drawer, and jeans and a shirt from the closet, before he went into the bath.

Showered, shaved and dressed, he was no longer quiet. He closed drawers with a bang, then looked at her. She was aware. He didn't lower his voice when he called his office from the bedside phone. He told his secretary that something had come up and he'd be late coming in. He said if he was needed, he'd be at his apartment. As he talked, his guest yawned and stretched.

After he hung up, he asked, "Are you awake, Hillary?" and watched her. She lay still, then she frowned briefly, but the frown slowly smoothed away as she went back into deeper sleep. He remembered how he'd slept after having taken just half of one of those pills, and he was six inches taller and a good fifty pounds heavier than she. She'd had a whole one. Dumb woman, taking someone else's pills.

He went into the kitchen, fed the cat and slammed pots around, making noise deliberately so that she could waken by herself in his bed. All of the civilized world knows that the mingling aromas of coffee and bacon can wake the dead. Angus prepared the combination expectantly.

She didn't come in; he listened, then he went to the bedroom and looked down at her. She sighed. Then she licked her lips in that maddening way she had. She ought to know that any woman sleeping in a man's bed should not do that.

She stretched marvelously, arching her back, then yawned. He and the cat watched, fascinated. She opened her eyes and looked around, completely disoriented. He waited. Her gaze came to him and she stared.

"Good morning, Goldilocks." He smiled and licked his own lips.

"Goldilocks?" She mumbled the question, still not very alert.

Her expression was vacant. He'd drawn a dummy? "My name is Behr. You're in my bed. You've heard of Goldilocks and the bear?"

"The *three* bears."

Well, at least she'd had the nursery stories. If she had that much memory, perhaps there'd be something to build on. He sighed. Then he smiled again. "There's only one bear here. My name is B-E-H-R, but it's pronounced 'bear.'"

Hillary looked at him with frowning astonishment. Where had he come from? He was tall, with dark straight hair and the greenest eyes she'd ever seen. He was magnificent. Shoulders. A great body. She began to smile, then quickly sobered as she remembered where she was and that this man was the man who was living with Tate. No, worse; with whom Tate was living. She asked, "Have you heard from Tate?"

And *he* had the gall to smile and ask, "Who's Tate?"

TWO

Hillary echoed the man's words indignantly. "'Who's Tate?' What do you *mean*, who is Tate! Out of sight, out of mind? How dare you!" Since he belonged to Tate, he was a non-man to Hillary, and in her temper she ignored the fact that he was there in the room and watching her.

With the cat sitting on the bed and listening with full attention, Hillary flipped back the sheet and swung long legs to the floor, stood and stormed over to her suitcase. Still irritated, she bent over and snatched out clean clothes before she straightened and turned toward him.

Angus's hands were in his jeans pockets, and he had one shoulder propped against the doorjamb. There was a little smile on his face as his quick glances went up and down and back and forth over her.

She demanded, "You have no idea where Tate is?"

He shook his head, his smile intact, his eyes still busily enjoying this new, frontal view of Hillary.

His avid expression finally sank into her consciousness, and she looked down at herself. Her breasts had peaked with her fury and were so obvious in that soft T-shirt that she abruptly turned around to jerk on jeans and a shirt over her sleeping outfit. When she faced him again, she was a little red-faced but still so angry with him that she was carried through any other embarrassment.

She took a deep breath as she buttoned the shirt and gave him a level look. "I don't understand how you could know Tate well enough for her to move in here, then be indifferent to the fact that she's been taken."

"Taken?" He frowned.

"You didn't know?"

"I don't even know Tate. So how could I know she'd been...taken? 'Taken' with what? Measles? Mumps? Who is she?"

"If you don't know her, as you claim, then what was she doing using this apartment?"

"She wasn't. This is solely mine." He folded his arms across his fine chest.

"Whose clothes are in that closet and in that drawer?"

"My, you were busy, weren't you."

"I was looking for her—" she should give no information to this stranger "—something."

"Well, her 'something' isn't here."

With fine hauteur, she told him in a diminishing way, "I'm surprised at you. You appear the hero type, yet here the woman you've obviously been living with is gone, and you claim not to know anything, not even who she is. I'm very disappointed in you, Mr. Behr, or whatever your name is. Bears are supposed to be brave and protective, but you're not either of those. You must be very disappointed in yourself when you look in the mirror."

He gave her a stern look. "Before you get up on your high horse, maybe we should comment on why you would take a codeine pill prescribed to me."

"Codeine?"

"Yes."

"Oh. I had no idea—"

"That's the point. You're not supposed to take other people's medications."

"I was exhausted, and my brain wouldn't quit—"

"If you'd taken much more, your brain could have stopped altogether."

"Well—"

"Who is Tate?"

She seized on that to refuel her depleted indignation. "As if you didn't know!"

"Assume that I don't, for I don't. Since we're in my apartment, you've broken in here and—"

"I had a key."

"Who the hell gave it to you?"

"*Tate.*"

"To this apartment? To apartment nine?"

"Nine? No. This one. Six."

"This is apartment *nine.* How did your key fit this lock?"

She strode long-legged and barefoot over to the front door, jerked it wide open and said, "See? Six." Her head was back, her other hand on her hip. Her whole attitude was of indignant defiance.

He looked at her thoughtfully, then strolled over toward her. She didn't give ground. Unthreateningly, he slowly reached past her and straightened the nine.

She stared at the nine as it slowly gave up, sliding back down into being a six. Her face changed in her surprise. He waited for an abject apology, but she said, "I've been all this time in the wrong place."

"Who is Tate, who lives in apartment six?"

"My sister."

"What's going on?"

"I don't know." She went to the bedroom, scooped up her suitcase in her arms, came back to the living room and crashed into his chest at the door. When he took the suitcase from her and jounced it to get everything inside and zipped it closed, she picked up her purse and shoes. She took her suitcase from him and started out the still-open door.

"Where you going?" he snapped.

"To find apartment six." How reasonable that was. What did he think she was going to do? "I have to call Carter."

He reached out to prevent her from slamming the door and followed her out into the hall. "Six is that way." He gestured.

She came back past him, ignoring his frown and the fact that he followed her.

In the lock of apartment six, Tate's key fit perfectly. Hillary opened the door, dumped her burdens onto the floor and made a beeline to the desk, which held Tate's computer. Hillary opened drawers and found the address book. In spite of Tate's having told her to wait, she flipped to C and found Carter. She punched out the number and waited. And waited. And waited as it rang. She saw there was no other name, just Carter. And there was no address.

Angus said by her shoulder, "I don't think he's there. He could be at work."

She seemed to wilt a little. Very carefully she put the receiver back into its cradle as the cat came along the hall and into number six with great curiosity.

Angus asked again, "What's going on?"

She put her hands to her face and rubbed it, then pushed her hair back, completely unaware that she was a woman with an attractive man. Until then. She looked up at him. Since now she knew he wasn't Tate's, she "saw" him. And she understood she'd been unkind to him. "I'm sorry I said all those things to you, Mr. Behr. I—"

"Angus."

"Angus. I couldn't understand how you could know Tate and not try to help her."

"You must realize by now that I don't know her. Who 'took' her? Have you called the police? What's going on?"

She shrugged. "I don't know. Tate said not to call the police."

"Why not?"

"It's a long story."

"Well..." He judged she really was a little frustrated and not very receptive to questioning right then. "Let's look around and see if there's anything that might be interesting or different."

They made a thorough search of the whole apartment. Tate had left a note on the refrigerator: "Hi, Beanpole. Welcome to the fast track. 78 RPM."

Angus gave Hillary another quick scan. He knew her curves were real, so he asked unbelievingly, "Beanpole?"

"I was a late bloomer."

They went on searching. It didn't take long. There were only three rooms and a bath. The bedroom, with Tate's neatly made bed, was large, and the kitchen was an efficient blocked-off corner. The living and dining areas were combined, and the view from the windows was absolutely marvelous as they faced Lake Michigan and the curving shore. Below was a marina with boats in rows along piers. There were some power boats, but mostly there were sailing boats with rocking "stick" masts.

When there was no other place to search—and that included the ice cubes—Angus gave Hillary an appraising look and advised, "You need to eat something. Did you have lunch yesterday?"

"No. I drove all night. I went to bed at your place about eleven yesterday morning."

"I'm going down to lock my door. When I come back, we'll see what Tate has in her refrigerator. Then we'll get sorted out." Then he said, "Let me in when I come back." It wasn't a question; he was telling her what to do.

She nodded, and he left, carefully trying the door after he'd closed it. He was back very quickly, and she hesitated, but she did open the door to him.

He hadn't been positive she would let him in, and he'd wondered what he would have to do in order to get back inside, so he was relieved to be on the same side of the door with her. He smiled at Hillary as if he'd expected her to admit him, and he carried the cold coffee and bacon into Tate's kitchen. It was then that he really understood that he'd committed himself to whatever was wrong about this Tate, who was her sister. And he did speculate on what in God's name he was wading into so blindly. His practical parents hadn't raised their little boy, Angus, to be rash.

Angus and Hillary, those intimate strangers, were a little awkward together. Angus took over the kitchen and fixed breakfast, while Hillary played back all the messages on the answering machine. She played it again, and they both listened intently. No ransom demands, no clues. No queer messages that could be misinterpreted. But among the messages was Hillary's "I'm on my way."

"That was you!"

"Yes. There was always the chance she might get back."

As Angus and the cat ate, Hillary just picked at the food on her plate. He inquired, "Why haven't you called the police?"

"Tate said to wait ten days. She thinks she'll be released soon. If she isn't, then I call the police."

"Why would anyone take her?"

"I don't know."

"Your sister. Where's she work?"

"The *People's Voice*."

"That's an erudite paper. No muckrakers. She a reporter?"

"She's editor of the women's page."

"Oh." He was surprised and just a little disappointed. "Well, that seems to eliminate that. I thought she might have stepped on somebody's toes."

"Tate is a good reporter. She *can* be stubborn. She's very principled, actually."

"Did she fire anybody?"

"I have no idea."

"If she's principled, she wouldn't be using or selling anything illegal, would she?"

"Of course not."

"Then how do you know she's in trouble?"

"I got a letter."

He gave her a *very* patient look. "As they dragged her out, she scribbled you a postcard in order to reach help, down in Kansas City, Missouri, via the U.S. Postal Service?"

"Whatever it was that involved her, she must have known it was chancy."

"When did you get the letter?"

"The day before yesterday."

"So she's been missing for at least three days. Let's call the police."

"She said to wait ten days."

"Do you have the letter? Let me see it."

Hillary went to her purse and brought the note back to the table. Even with him reading it aloud, the words were still the same. Nothing had changed. Angus's voice was pleasantly deep and slow as he read the text:

"'If you get this letter, I'm probably being held somewhere. Don't panic. I'm sure I'm not in any danger. But if you haven't heard from me in ten days, get in touch with Carter. Don't call the police, and don't tell the family. Yet. I love you, Boy. Tate.'"

"Beanpole" had been bad enough, so now Angus was incredulous: "'Boy?'"

"We were five daughters. Dad named us all girls' names that were rather masculine: Tate, Fredricka, Georgina, Roberta, and Hillary. Tate was the tomboy, and they played Tarzan. I was too young to *be* anything, so I was Boy."

Angus nodded. Her family sounded a little weird to him.

They didn't say anything for a while, then Angus commented, "Dead policemen's souls must twist every time that 'Don't call the cops' phrase is used." And his glance spoke his criticism.

"I've got to get in touch with Carter." She looked at her watch. "It won't hurt anything to just call him and say I'm in town. He might know something. I'll call for him at the paper in a while. He might work there. It seems logical. Their switchboard won't be open yet. I wonder why Carter doesn't answer his home number. It's too early for him to have left for work."

"Maybe 'they' took him, too."

"Why would you say that?"

"If he knows all about this and what you should do, his knowing would put him in the same boat as Tate."

"Yes."

"Is Carter his first or last name?"

"I don't know."

"What's it say in her book?"

"Just Carter. No other name and no address."

"Call information and see if you can get the address."

Hillary immediately went to the phone and did just that. The operator's supervisor explained that since it was an unlisted number, no information or address could be given. Only those names or numbers already in the directory were available through the operator.

Hillary hung up and sat down to look at Angus. Then, a little critically, Angus suggested, "Why not just wait? Tate ought to know what she's doing."

Hillary shook her head, frowning. "I'll call the paper. Maybe he'll be there, or Tate's secretary will know how to reach him. I'm sure this is going to turn out to be simple and everything will be all right."

They sat, not speaking. Angus was skeptical. He was an insurance investigator, and he knew people weren't always as nice as those Hillary had probably known. She looked like someone on whom Life smiled and made her path an easy one. A sound riveted their attention to the living room. It was the cat who was on the back of the sofa, looking at a minimum-size fish mounted on a very large plaque on the wall. It was a rainbow trout on a plaque large enough to accommodate a deep-sea sailfish.

Angus questioned, "Who caught the fish?"

"That must be the one Tate caught. She was in Canada last month and that was the first legal-size fish she'd ever caught, so she had it mounted. Isn't it ridiculous? How like Tate to do that."

Angus grinned, and his mental picture of Tate became clearer.

They watched as the cat went around investigating everything. In the silence, Hillary asked, "What's your cat's name?"

"Cat."

"That's all?"

"When I moved in, the cat was already there."

"Someone just . . . left it?"

"Her."

"It's rude not to name her."

Expansively, he declared, "You name her, and you've got yourself a cat!"

"How long have you had her?"

"She's had me for two months now."

"You've lived here two months and you've never met Tate? You must be in your dotage."

"You have a great talent for setting me down hard. The reason I don't know Tate is probably because our schedules never meshed." Then, with some smug calculation he offered, "You can introduce me to her."

Her quick, protesting breath intake parted her lips just a little before she turned her head away, but it was enough to soothe his ego. She was feeling a touch of possessiveness? Well, so was he. There was just something about spending a night in bed with a woman that raised a man's territorial feelings. He vividly recalled holding her against him. He smiled a little as he cast a glance down her body and found he had to shift on his chair.

She tried Carter's number again, and again the phone only rang. She set the receiver back in its cradle and moved around restlessly.

"Why push it?" Angus said. "Wait and see. Tate said wait ten days. This is only the third day since you got her note, and she doesn't think there's any danger."

"I'm just going to tell Carter I'm in town. That way he'll know where to find me."

There was a disapproving silence, then Angus suggested, "Wait a week."

Changing the subject, she asked him, "What do you do for a living? Aren't you supposed to be working on a weekday? You must work if you can afford to live here on the lake, in an apartment that has this same panoramic view. We don't have anything like this in Kansas City.''

The jumble of comments made him realize she was filling the silence, inviting him to talk in order to distract her, so he complied. "I'm a maritime insurance investigator for a company that deals in that field.''

"The sea?''

"And lakes. All claims are based on admiralty law. Marine loss problems are a separate field. Lost cargo, which ship, who lost it. Freight insurance cost, whether the seller or buyer pays the insurance. I know boats.'' He cocked his head and added, "Boats are the name for anything that can be lifted onto a ship. A ship is big. I also know people.'' He took a deep, reluctant breath and committed himself firmly. "If we can't get hold of Carter and you are adamantly opposed to sensibly calling the cops, I know some people we can call on for help.''

She turned a surprised look to him. "I appreciate that.'' She'd just realized he'd thrown in his lot with hers, and it touched her very much. Not that she needed him, but it was nice of him to offer his help.

Decisively, since he was used to control, he stated firmly, "I would like to call the police now.''

She shook her head. "Not yet.''

"In all the time you wait, you lose valuable memories of the people who might have noticed something... different.''

"I know. I look for stolen children.''

"In reports I've read that in this country only about twenty kids a year are actually stolen by a stranger. That's too many, but most of the rest are runaways or those taken by the divorced parent who didn't get custody.''

"How would you like to have a child somewhere in the world, growing up, and never seeing him or her? Never getting a letter. Or a phone call. Or a picture. Nothing. Holding a vigil on his birthday, alone, wondering where he is. Not even sure the child is still alive. Or if he misses you. Or if he remembers you. Or if he knows you love him."

"Yeah, I see. I never thought of the kid, only the quarreling parents." He thought for a minute before he added, "... Who are so childish."

"Selfish," she corrected him.

"So. What do you plan to do while you wait to hear from your sister?"

Stubbornly she replied, "I'll call Carter."

Restlessly he rose and paced around, as nosy as the cat who jumped up on the table by Hillary.

Hillary lifted the cat to the floor with a scolding "No!" Then she scolded Angus, "Why haven't you taught your cat not to get on the table?"

"She was in the apartment before I was, and she treats me like a guest. Under those circumstances, how can I correct her?" He had by then uncovered Tate's computer, and, forgetting about the cat's lack of discipline, he said, "It's compatible to mine. I know you don't want to come to my place to wait—Tate might call here—so do you mind if I bring some stuff over to work on here? And may I give this number?"

"Sure."

"Did your key really fit my door?"

"Yes. It was a little stiff, but my lock in Kansas City is stiff, so I didn't pay any attention."

"May I try it?" That way, he thought, he'd be able to get into her apartment if she decided she didn't want him back.

Without hesitating, she took the key from her purse and handed it to Angus. He smiled at her. As he accepted the key, he knew she had accepted him.

With brisk busyness, Angus used the versatile key, which fit smoothly, as he came back inside. "It worked on my door," he commented with a grin. Then he tried his own key on her door, but it would not work even with considerable coaxing; however, Tate's key had worked again on his door lock.

Hillary shook her head. "It's a good thing we're not sneak thieves. We could go around trying all the other locks."

"Now, that's an idea. There's a blonde who walks by in a languishing way that . . ." But he stopped.

As the minute stretched, Hillary asked with just a tinge of sharpness, "That . . . what?"

"Hmm?" He raised his thick brows in the most innocent way. But he didn't wait for her to re-form her question. He carried a folder over to settle himself at Tate's desk and activate her computer.

Hillary followed him and punched out Carter's number on the desk phone. Again, it only rang. In this day and time, why didn't this Carter have an answering machine?

She knew that Angus watched her as she replaced the phone and turned away. It was still too early to call the business office at the paper. She looked around at Tate's apartment, seeing the familiar things her sister had always had, and she again felt a nagging concern for Tate.

Worrying wouldn't help. Hillary needed to be busy to pass the time, so she cleared the table and scrubbed out the clean kitchen. Then she showered, put on a beige summer cotton dress with a dark brown belt and slid into moccasins. She brushed her thick blond hair until it crackled before she tamed it down and coiled it on top of her head. For something else to do, she added makeup rather sparingly.

She sorted her own clothes, shook out the hanging ones and put them in Tate's closet. She hesitated, then touched the shoulder of a familiar jacket. Where was Tate? Who had her? Why?

She opened a lingerie drawer, and there were no red wispy things like those in Angus's drawer. Hillary put her modest but wildly colored underwear in a corner of Tate's drawer. As she put her makeup on the dresser, her glance rested on the small bottle sitting there. She took up Tate's perfume to hold it in her hand. Finally she set it precisely back in place.

In a mirror on the living-room wall, Angus could see Hillary's reflection in the bedroom mirror, and he witnessed her distraction. He'd known he could watch because there were identically placed mirrors in his own apartment.

Hillary came back to the living room and in her restlessness began to tidy the audiotapes unaccountably disarranged on a shelf. Then she recalled the "78 RPM" on Tate's note and paid closer attention. One was labeled "Boy." She put it into the nearby tape player. She thought "Boy" could be the English rock star Boy George, or it might be a message about Carter! But it was Tate recording a letter to Hillary.

It began, "Since you now have a Walkman—"

And Hillary said in an aside, "Where did Tate get that idea?"

That caught Angus's attention, and he said, "Listen!"

"—I thought we could exchange thoughts this way. Phoning isn't always convenient or reliable. I've been thinking of our childhood, Boy, and I wonder how much of it you remember. The sharing of such memories can be so important to a family."

Angus was riveted. "She's trying to tell you something. Listen."

The sound was perfect. It was as if Tate were right there. But Tate's voice droned on in seemingly random memories. Boring. The tape lasted about twenty minutes.

Angus said thoughtfully, "Tate is smart. While she believes she's safe enough, there must be some reason she's not altogether sure. The note proves that. So the tape could be a planting of clues that would help to find her if she isn't released on time. We have to be alert. Let's call the police."

Hillary shook her head impatiently but called Carter again. Then again. And finally she could call the paper's business office. No one named Carter worked there, and Tate's secretary was out sick. "May I have her number? This is Tate's sister."

The voice replied, "Tate isn't in today. And we don't give out numbers. Too many weirdos running around loose. Sorry."

As she put the phone down, unsuccessful yet again, Angus demanded, "Tell me."

"Her secretary is sick today. No Carter works there." She sighed. "They said Tate isn't in today."

"Okay. That does it. We should call the police."

"She specifically asked me not to," Hillary protested.

"I could call a couple of friends. Just to get a start on this."

Very reluctantly, she said, "All right. But I ought to call her friends first and continue to call Carter. He must be back sometime. Tate gave no particular time to call, just said to call him. He could work out of his apartment or house."

"Give me a detailed description of Tate."

"She's five eight, brunette, thirty-five, beautiful. Blue eyed. Very kind. A nice figure. She stands straight. Confident. After her divorce she took back our family name, Lambert." It seemed strange to describe Tate under such circumstances. Unreal. They were searching for Tate.

"After we get in touch with my friends, I think we'd better start hunting Carter," Angus said.

"Where?"

"The hospitals, jails, morgue..."

Hillary said, "Oh."

"Yes. Tate did contact you. You're her ace in the hole. But we need to find Carter."

"Thank you, Angus."

"Not yet. But we'll try to see what we can do."

Three

———

Y"ou're very kind to want to help, but I do know what I'm doing," Hillary assured Angus.

She was turning him down? Angus shot a look at her. So she was one of the independent ones; he found he was a little offended. This was his cue to back out. He didn't have the time for this puzzle of a missing sister anyway. He didn't need the hassle. He drew a breath to say the words to release himself from her and the situation—and he saw that she was waiting for his reply.

He figured that if she waited for him to argue with her, she must be dealing with the fact that she needed him. Did he want to give his time and effort? Or did he want to take the opportunity and slip out of this complication? She was giving him the chance... and she wasn't breathing as she waited for his answer.

He considered her. As contrary as she might be, she was very feminine. Women were somewhat limited as to what they could do in any dangerous investigative work, in that they were so vulnerable. If Tate didn't show up again and they had to hunt for her, it could be very dangerous. And men noticed any young woman. Every man who met her would notice Hillary. She might need him.

He casually shifted his feet to disguise the fact that his glance checked her out again before he looked back to her face. She was a very tasty-looking woman. She moved nicely. Her voice was pleasant, and she smelled good. He thought of her in his arms last night, there in his bed, and the whole front of his body remembered her vividly.

To get her to agree to accept his help—which she must have realized she might need—it would take tact. In a placating, coaxing manner he began, "An investigator can always use some help. If you don't hear from your sister in this next week, there's a lot of work to be done, so many things to check out that you could use us. We could save you time. Just tell us what you want done."

Already giving in, she said with the right amount of hesitation, "I don't like to impose."

She was so transparent, leading him on to coax her. He could read her like a book. Very soberly, Angus assured her in the expected way, "I would like to help. I believe this could be interesting. And the people I know would feel left out if we didn't include them. They're sharp. They might even have ideas of their own to contribute." Inside his head, Angus heard them laugh at that little understatement. They would attack this problem with an avalanche of suggestions. They had fantastic imaginations.

"Well . . . all right."

"Thank you!" He even smiled as if in triumph.

But then she surprised him. She took a deep, relieved breath and said, "Oh, I'm so glad. Most of the time I can stand back mentally and think clearly, but I am worried about Tate. I needed to be sure you really didn't mind."

He grinned. He meant only to pat her shoulder but she turned against his chest, and he held her, his steely nerves and rigid muscles keeping his comforting "brotherly." His thoughts weren't at all brotherly. He'd never been so taken with any other woman. Why her? It seemed so urgent for him to hold her. So sweet and natural. He wanted to take her to bed and comfort her the way all men want to do with a troubled woman, in the only logical way.

By the time he could release her, his sexual tension had filmed his body and his breath was a little harsh. When this hunt was over, she would owe him one. Maybe a couple. A couple of couplings? It would be an additional goal. That rather surprised Angus, because he really wasn't a man for casual sex. He decided it was because "Goldilocks" had been sleeping in his bed. Yes. She had certainly been there, all right. With him.

He slowly extricated himself from her, in a very gradual way, so that she thought it was she who withdrew. He smiled his wicked smile down at her and said, "Everything will come out okay. Wait and see. We'll just get in a little groundwork while we wait."

He directed, "You call all the hospitals and see if there are any Carters as patients. Especially if any are there from injuries. Make a list of each name and hospital, and we'll check them out after we have lunch. I'll go back to my apartment and call some friends. We'll meet with them here tonight." His adding "Okay?" wasn't for permission; it was a do-you-understand one.

"And the morgue?"

"Ask only for those who died unnaturally. Say you were supposed to meet someone named Carter for your sister. That you've lost the paper with the full name and can't get in touch with your sister for a week. Give your and Tate's real names. We might have to get permission to question or search if there are any dead Carters." Then he took a deep breath and asked her very carefully, very seriously, "Hillary, we might have to go to the police anyway. Why not now?"

"I do know that, but there must have been a reason Tate said I should wait."

He gave her a slight grin and put a hand on her shoulder to slowly waggle it just a little. "Loyalty is a good trait, but it does get in the way here. I *urge* that we contact the police as soon as possible. We need them."

It cost her to shake her head, and she did it very regretfully.

"Then, if not now, promise your permission if nothing turns up today. You'll be calling Carter in between the other calls, right?"

"Yes."

"Promise me. Tomorrow will be the fourth day."

"Yes."

But he didn't leave it at that; he pushed: "How about this evening?"

She really wanted to agree, but she could only say, "We'll see."

"After I call my friends, I'm going to get a run-down on any offbeat activities that would warrant a temporary hostage." He was thinking on his feet, speaking his thoughts. "Something that's coming off." His voice was almost gentle.

He went over and looked out along the curving lakeshore. Musingly he went on, "Something that Tate was seen to have witnessed, or information she's known to have. It would have to be something public that appears one way but could turn out another way if the real or additional facts were known."

Angus turned back toward Hillary and said, "That's the only thing that could be involved. That *must* be so in this case. The note proves it. If this were a regular snatch, it would have been a surprise. But Tate *knew* she might be taken, and either she was going to move on what she knew or else she needed more information and was digging for it. We'll find out where she was looking."

Hillary said softly, "This is different from looking for stolen children."

He nodded, then shrugged. "Admiralty law is different from all others. Maritime insurance is different from life or car or liability. Doctors practice in and on different parts of the body. There are cops who specialize in snatchings. Let's call the cops who know about this sort of thing. By the time that letter was mailed and you got it, at least three days had elapsed. This could already be the sixth or seventh day."

"This evening," she acquiesced, but her voice was uncertain.

He shook his head once in exasperation, but he said, "Let's get busy."

Hillary went to punch out Carter's number yet again, and Angus stood and watched her. No reply. As she put the phone back, she turned to look at him in such a way that he was drawn to her. He kept the kiss brotherly but only just barely.

He saw to it the door was locked after him, and went on to his own apartment, leaving the cat with Hillary. He entered his place, locked the door and called the police. "Paul? Angus. I've got a peculiar situation here."

Disgruntled, Paul asked, "Now what?"

"For once, I don't deserve that. I've got what might be a very interesting puzzler. I'm calling Jim, and how about Willie? This is a strange deal." And he proceeded to tell Paul the little he knew, and that—due to the fact that he was a cop and Hillary had been told not to call one—Paul could only contact Hillary that evening when they gathered in Tate's apartment.

Paul groused in a nasty way, "How kind you are to give me this...cutting edge."

"I knew you'd be grateful."

"Willie, huh."

"I thought that'd perk up your ears. It's been a while since she told you to take off, hasn't it? Do you suppose she's calmed down yet? That was one of your nobler moments."

Paul said a shocking string of words.

"Good, get it out of your system now, before you see Willie. She'd wash your mouth out with soap. If you cleaned up your mouth, you might be able to speak up in polite society and you wouldn't have to sit there silently and seem so stupid."

Paul made another observation.

"*Tsk, tsk, tsk.* You're lucky I knew my Uncle Fred before I ever met you, or my little ears might be singed."

With almost artistic crudeness, Paul suggested some interesting things for Angus to do with his ears.

Angus laughed.

Hillary found there are many more than several hospitals in a city the size of Chicago, and then there are those in the outlying districts. Even with diligent calling, Hillary didn't get half of them phoned. But of those she did contact, Carters hadn't had a fortunate week, and there were a number who were in the hospital through no effort of their own.

At lunch, Hillary read her list to Angus as they ate peanut-butter sandwiches in his apartment—with the cat on the table. Hillary sternly removed her three times.

Angus protested, "It's her apartment. She ought to be able to sit on the table in her own apartment."

"I shudder to think how undisciplined your children will be."

"Marriage terrifies me," he confessed cheerfully.

She said with prim approval, "At least you feel that your children should be legitimate."

"Absolutely. But I believe I'll pass on marriage and therefore on children. There are more than enough in this world."

Hillary watched her fingers toy with her sandwich. "There are a lot of very unhappy marriages."

"You would see all of those." He nodded and chewed awhile before he added, "Doesn't it bother you that you might be helping the wrong parent?"

"On occasion. Generally both are basically right. In their own ways each is very concerned for the child or children."

He scoffed cynically, "So they divorce and quarrel over them? That hardly makes sense."

"I've found it's easy to be critical from the inside of a cocoon."

"You're assuming that I know nothing about marriage or divorce?"

"Do you?" She raised her stern gaze to his eyes.

"I'm the youngest and, like you, a tagalong. I have nieces and nephews close to my age. All my brothers have good marriages. The kids are secure and thriving, and so are the wives."

"So the Behr men know how to treat women?"

"Barefoot and pregnant." He raised his head and gave her a smug look through half-closed eyes as he treated her to an asininely attractive, arrogantly male grin.

She shook her head in disgust, but she could not quite prevent a ghost of an answering smile.

He bit off another quarter of one of his sandwiches and shifted it over into his cheek before he asked, "Where do we start?" Then he chewed as he waited for her reply.

"You're the one who knows Chicago. How do we plot this?"

He swallowed, licked his lips and told her, "I have a map. I'm a native of five years' residence."

"You're a native in five years? To be a native in Missouri, it takes a good twenty years. But it takes only six months in Alaska; then you get a share of the oil profits."

"I have a brother who moved to Texas, and it only took two hours," he told her.

"I think Texas is mental. Your brother probably bought a pair of cowboy boots in Oklahoma before he crossed the border."

"Now, how could you have known that?"

"Or you can be blond. There are a lot of blondes in Texas." She threw that in.

"Somebody take you for a native?"

"I went to Odessa, and someone asked me for directions as I came out of the airport."

"That's no test," he scoffed. "Any place would claim you."

Hillary gave a glance to acknowledge his compliment. "Actually the Lamberts have been in Texas for a very long while, down near Kerrville. Tate's been here in Chicago almost five years." But she had said it before she remembered the incredible fact that Tate was missing, and Hillary looked off out the window at the masts rocking in the motion of the restless lake.

Angus didn't misunderstand. "We'll find her."

"Let's go."

"After you eat at least half of the sandwich. It's going to be a long afternoon."

"Should we split up? We could cover twice the territory."

"I notice you have two Carters at Billings. We'll go there first. One is here at— We may need a couple of days to go through this. We have to be back here for supper. We can pick up something and bring it home. My friends are coming tonight. Paul, Jim and Willie. Willie's a girl...uh...a woman."

"I do believe I've heard a nod toward equal rights from you, Mr. Behr."

"I try to keep all feathers smoothed."

"How clever of you," she replied. But he grinned that dangerous male grin of his, and she felt something like fear slip up through her insides. Only it wasn't terror; it was more a...delicious fear. She sat still, trying to decide what it was.

"If you're positive you don't want that other half sandwich, I'll force myself. But you *have* to eat the rest of that half."

"It'll stick in my throat," she protested.

"It'll absorb, and you need the nourishment." He said it as if she ought to know something that basic.

Leaving the cat in his apartment, they set out on a very interesting odyssey. It hadn't occurred to them that Carter might be a woman. There was a woman at Billings who had been in a car wreck. But that had happened before Tate mailed the letter, so that Carter couldn't be the one Tate meant.

At Memorial Hospital there was a man in a coma. He'd been beaten. He was the age of someone Tate might know. But there was a woman with him, and when they asked the woman if he knew a Tate Lambert, she became hostile. "Just how did this Tate...get acquainted with my man? Who is this...who's after Frank? Just let a man get helpless and all sorts of...turns up to claim him. This Tate had better not come around, or she'd look a lot different afterwards. And..."

They eased away with the woman still hollering. The man on the bed never moved.

At eight hospitals that afternoon, they told their plotted story of missing a meeting with an unknown Carter. It was tough to see so many Carters having such a rough time. One watched them suspiciously through their explanation and questioned, "You're from the IRS, right? You get me down, sick in bed, and you attack, right? Well, you ain't got one damned thing on me. I'm clean. Why don't you go . . ."

Since there was no possible way they could actually do that, the couple left in the middle of his directions. And as they walked back to the parking garage for Angus's car, he said thoughtfully, "It's a great country, isn't it? Where else could citizens abuse officials the way people do here in these United States?"

"But we aren't officials."

"They don't know that."

"That's true."

There wasn't one plausible candidate for Tate's Carter. And although Hillary tried between each visit, the real Carter still didn't answer the phone.

It was a long, hard day, and Hillary was dragging her heels by the time they got back to Tate's apartment. The lake breeze was marvelous, and they opened up the windows to hear the city birds and to listen to the sounds of the traffic.

Being on the second floor with the windows open to the lake breeze was very nice. The feeling of freedom the open windows gave them on that hot summer day overrode the noise from the cars and people in and by the pool.

Carter still didn't answer his ringing phone.

"I invited our associates to come here to Tate's. Let's eat supper at my place. I have a freezer stacked with frozen dinners, and a microwave, so it's no sweat. You can leave the windows open here, if you like, but be sure the door's locked when you come over. Why don't you soak in a nice deep bath for a while? My mother always does that when things are stressful. It apparently helps."

"Thank you."

"Want me to scrub your back?" he offered with an earnest, helpful-citizen expression. "I'm a raw novice, but I'd be willing to learn."

"No, thanks."

"Put on some shorts," he suggested. "I'm going to have a shower. Have you any particular things you don't like to eat?"

"I'm not really hungry."

"After your bath you'll be ravenous. Shall I surprise you?" He grinned as he plotted all sorts of surprises.

"Whatever you're having."

"I like an easy woman."

She raised a lofty gaze to his face as she said, "I'm not an easy woman."

"Well, darn." His voice was mild, and his grin was naughty. "Your key works on my door, so come on down when you're ready."

She nodded as he went out of the apartment, and she heard him close the door and try it to be sure it was locked. Hillary looked around rather vapidly, then trudged into the bedroom and set out clothes. She did soak in a deep tub, and it did help.

Dressed in a dark cotton pullover and shorts, she brushed her hair and left it loose. She paused and paid attention to the feeling that tingled through her. Anticipation at the thought of being with Angus again.

She used her key in his door, and it opened with the usual coaxing. The cat greeted her, glad for company. Hillary inquired, "Been on the table all afternoon?"

The cat blinked as if with humor.

"Or did you trade off being on the table with sitting on the kitchen counter?"

The cat complimented her intelligence, marking Hillary as her territory by rubbing her chin on Hillary's ankles.

Straightening from petting the cat, Hillary heard the shower. She realized Angus was standing in there, naked, under the water's spray. How could she think of Angus's body when her sister was missing? She tried to blank out Angus's body with Tate's face; but she could not, so to distract herself she set the table. That took only two minutes, so she tried Carter's number. Again she was unsuccessful.

The cat jumped up onto one of the open windowsills and watched outside. Hillary went to the cat and petted it as she, too, stared out at the lake. She heard the shower shut off, and in her mind she watched Angus get out of the shower and begin to dry himself. Her hand lingered on the fur of the cat's back, toying with it.

He came from the bedroom, barefoot, pulling a navy T-shirt over his head. For a minute she saw his wide, tanned, hairy chest. He wore cream-colored shorts, and she saw that his hairy, muscular legs were brown. He was an outdoor man. As his head came through the neck of the T-shirt, he saw her and his green eyes lit with pleasure. "There you are," he said with satisfaction. That was exactly the sound, she mused. He was "satisfied" she was there.

He continued, "I chose a light chicken à la king for you. Something easy to digest. Does that sound good to you? Mary Jane, who lives on the fifth floor, has been darling in providing me with homemade bread

every week." He smiled like a lazy, green-eyed Chesh-
ire cat.

Hillary stared stonily at him and wondered quite
nastily just what Angus provided Mary Jane in return
for the bread.

Angus toasted the slices and poured the hot chicken
mixture over the buttered pieces. He set the food on
the table, and Hillary put the cat on the floor twice.
Angus didn't appear to notice, but he did feed the cat
before he sat down.

Sourly, Hillary realized Mary Jane's homemade
bread was perfect. Exactly the right moisture to survive the toasting, to remain crisp under the chicken
concoction, yet chewy and moist inside. It was delicious. Certain she was making a great impression on
St. Peter, who keeps track of all conduct and marks it
down in his book, Hillary said to Angus, "The bread
is perfect."

"Isn't it?" He grinned cheerily, but then he added,
"Mary Jane...isn't."

While she knew St. Peter couldn't possibly have
approved of Angus saying that, Hillary loved it. If she
was there long enough after they found Tate, Hillary
would have to find a man for Mary Jane. It was the
only fair thing to do.

But as she thought that, Hillary was aware that she
was staking her own claim on Angus. Really? She
glanced up and met his green-eyed wickedness. It was
exactly as if he could read her mind. Surely not. There
was no possible way for him to know she was attracted to him or that she had "seen" him naked in the
shower as he'd bathed and dried off. No way at all.

As they ate Mary Jane's perfect bread, Angus told
Hillary about the people who were coming there in a

very short while. "They're friends. Around my age. I'm thirty. We've worked together before this. All are investigators." Well, Paul could be termed that. "And Willie is something special. She's a psychologist, but she's something of a psychic, too. A weird woman."

He was silent as he chewed, then he went on to explain, "She and Paul were, uh, close, at one time, but he tried to box her in. Possessive. He got out of hand at a gathering where some man and Willie were in a psychic meeting of their minds that was apparently quite absorbing and something that Paul misunderstood. He got nasty. Willie blew up—being a female, she has a dreadful temper—and it was a very interesting evening for the rest of us. Paul has been licking his wounds ever since."

"Females have dreadful tempers?"

"Out of all that conversation, you chose that particular phrase?"

"It did stand out."

"Don't you worry about poor Paul?"

"No."

"He's really suffered. He loves her."

"Oh." Hillary's mind had been so busy with his story that she'd cleared her plate. She buttered another piece of Mary Jane's bread and added some grape jelly. She bit into it with jealous pleasure before she said, "But if Willie doesn't care for Paul, how will it help to get them together tonight?"

"She worships him. She just gets mad and backs herself into a corner, and he has no tact at all. We've been trying to think of a way to force them into seeing each other, and Tate's problem is the perfect thing."

With great irony, Hillary said, "How nice Tate could help."

"Now, Hillary, you know good and well we're going to find Tate, and it will probably be because we've snared Paul and Willie."

"I hope so."

"Wait and see. I'm always right," he assured her.

"How can you sit there and blandly make such a statement?"

He looked surprised. "It's true. Why be falsely modest? I suppose you've never admitted you're gorgeous."

"I'm not."

"I hate a liar."

"I'm pretty." She said it, rather nobly honest.

"Well, that's about the feeblest comment I've ever heard. That's like saying Mary Jane's bread passes muster."

Hillary smiled, then the laugh bubbled. He was delighted and laughed with her. But she said, "And you never say you're good-looking?"

He was astonished. "I am?"

"Angus!"

He got up and went to the living-room mirror to search his face intently. Then he shook his head and came back to the table to lift the cat to the floor as he sat down. "I might have known you'd lie. Women are flatterers."

"You are outrageous."

"Well, yes, since we're being honest. Are you engaged or in love or anything dumb?"

She shook her head.

"Have you been married?"

She shook it again.

"Me either."

"Whose clothing is in your bedroom?" She tilted back her head and narrowed her eyes.

"An old, longtime friend. That's past. I haven't figured what to do with those things yet. An anonymous donation to Goodwill?" He smiled, amused by the idea.

"How 'past'?"

"Very."

"Oh." She smiled a little.

He grinned back. "That clears the decks. Do you know one of those boats down there is mine? Do you sail? I suppose not in Missouri."

"We have lakes in Missouri and in eastern Kansas, and the Missouri River's no creek."

"Ah, so you do sail."

"No."

"We'll work on it. Let's see your muscle."

She pulled up her arm, rather proud of the slight bulge, which his thumb and two opposing fingers squashed with no effort at all.

"Not bad!" He complimented her on her muscle. "We'll make you a deckhand in no time. It's good for the character."

"I happen to know that crewing is an exhausting job."

"That's why it's good for the character—you keep working even when you know you must be dead."

The last word was an unfortunate one, he realized. It seemed to shiver ominously in the air between them, and he couldn't think of anything to say to get rid of it. Until then, Hillary's attention had only been caught on Tate as missing. But ... what if ...

Hillary pushed back her empty plate as if rejecting the food. She didn't even notice it was empty. But the

cat chose that time to jump back up on the table, and
Hillary lifted her down again with another sharp
"No!" But that wasn't the kind of word that could
dispel the word *dead*.

They carried the plates into the kitchen, and Angus
did talk, but it wasn't demanding of her attention and
she ignored him. She had become silent and somber.
She tried Carter's number, but he still didn't answer.

They washed the dishes by hand, since Angus had
decided she needed something to do, and he handed
her the broom and let her sweep the floor. It needed it.

Finally there was nothing left to do but go to Tate's
apartment and wait for the others to arrive. Hillary
picked up the cat and carried it along.

"Why are you taking her with us?"

"She'd be lonesome alone." Hillary walked on
ahead, unaware of Angus's thoughtful expression.

He collected the cat's litter box, then he followed
more slowly, watching Hillary. She cared about
whether a cat could be lonesome. She was a compassionate woman. He smiled. She might be convinced to
ease *his* loneliness... his hungers, in his way. He
whistled between his teeth, almost soundlessly.

Four

They went into Tate's apartment and Angus said, "Just watch—Paul will get here first. He'll want to watch Willie when she comes in the door and first sees him."

"She doesn't know Paul is going to be here?" Hillary was a little indignant. "You should have told her."

Angus shrugged and said the obvious. "She wouldn't have agreed to come."

"I'm not sure I like the idea that you set her up for such a surprise, with such calculation, and that you anticipate their meeting here."

He was offended. "I didn't do anything of the sort! All I did was ask some friends to come help us out. It doesn't have anything to do with how they feel about each other. They're adults; they can handle it. And I can hardly wait to see how they act!"

"You could have told Willie. Then she would be prepared, braced. She could have thought up how she'd react and what she'd say."

"Rehearse?" He pretended amazement as he quite nicely carried on the disagreement in order to distract her while she waited.

She gave him a chilly look. "If one is prepared, one doesn't make a fool of oneself."

"Oh? One does that, does one?"

"Don't mock me."

"I was being just as formal as 'one,' and just as snippy. Your eyes really sparkle when you laugh or when you're mad. Did you know that?"

She looked into his mesmerizing emerald pools of humor and forgot what they were talking about.

They heard the knock on the door and thought it was for the first time. Angus touched her nose and whispered, "Paul." Then he walked over, peered through the peephole, opened the door with a flourish and said, "Paul."

Hillary thought instantly that Paul walked like a cop. Now, why had she thought that? How many cops had she studied in order to make such a decision? None. But he walked like a cop. Dangerously. Angus hadn't mentioned what Paul did for a living, but she bet it wasn't insurance.

Paul was a little bulkier than Angus. Paul's shoulders were heavier; his body was just a little thicker. He was someone to hide behind. Like Angus, Paul could take care of any problem, she could tell. Angus had been right in calling on this one to help.

Paul came into the apartment slowly, which made Hillary wonder about the places he ordinarily entered...and why. With seemingly casual glances around, Paul didn't miss a thing. That included everything about Hillary. He didn't smile. He acknowledged the introduction to Hillary with a solemn nod. She saw that he wasn't a chatterer. Even social conversation must be tough for him. He could probably use a little therapy. Loosen him up. His behavior now was intimidating. No wonder he and Willie were having problems.

Angus asked Paul, "How've you been? Uh, Paul! Can you say anything?"

Paul gave Angus a stony look.

Angus explained to Hillary, "Paul is so foul-mouthed that he can't speak in front of ladies. He gets tongue-tied, because he's terrified what he'll say.

Paul glowered.

Angus went on, "He can only talk politely when he has a pencil and pad in his hands. That triggers something in his brain that he's speaking to 'citizens,' and then he speaks in a normal, acceptable way."

Politely cautious, Hillary inquired of Paul, "Are you an insurance investigator, too?"

Angus laughed, and after a slight pause and a murderous glare at Angus, Paul said a terse "Sorta."

Angus cheered the pristine word as Jim arrived. They all greeted one another.

Hillary said, "How do you do?"

And Jim smiled as he shook her hand. He was laid-back, casual and sleepy eyed.

Hillary thought Jim was probably spaced-out. With all the media blitz on drugs and so many people suffering fried brains from using the stuff, Hillary was surprised that Jim would indulge, or that the others would tolerate it. None of the others gave Jim one piercing or condemning glance. So she gave him a stiff, censoring one.

And at last Willie tapped on the door and was admitted. She was rather mousy looking and cool. Her hair was short and carelessly tumbled, as if she had just impatiently brushed it aside. Her clothing was of a blah color and the style nondescript, but the material was soft and clingy. She wore no makeup, which left her face shiny. She smiled like a violet. Soft, tender and fragile. She said "Hello," and the word floated like a balm over the room. The men smiled as if the balm had touched all the hurt places in their egos and souls.

Hillary became bristly and moved closer to Angus.

Angus was aware of the move and enormously pleased. He gave her an unseen sideways grin and put an arm around her shoulders as he said, "This is Hillary Lambert, Willie. You two are like peas in a pod."

That jolted Hillary. Angus thought she was like this natural, magic woman?

Willie took Hillary's hand and looked at her with intense concentration. Hillary felt her soul being observed. Was Willie really psychic or just a very clever psychologist?

Willie told her, "As soon as I heard this was about a Tate and her sister was named Hillary, I knew we had an entire lineage in common. Our masculine-oriented ancestors must meld back a way."

That showed a sensitivity that went beyond knowledge, Hillary thought. "Angus told me you're psychic." She said that in the way people do who are very impressed.

Shrugging it off, Willie explained, "I sometimes 'know' things or feel them. It's really just a hunch.

Nothing dramatic. Once or twice I've made an impressive guess that's curled the guys' hair and turned out right. They've been so impressed those couple of times that they forget all the wrong hunches."

Hearing the candid words, Hillary realized Willie was an unusual woman. A little strange. Her words had been normal as she'd reassured Hillary she was ordinary. How like an oddity to soothe nervous people. But her assurances showed that Willie was in tune with the rest of humanity. She knew people need to think everything is stable. She'd probably fool most. Very quietly Hillary whispered, "Paul's here."

Willie's voice was calm. "I know."

Hillary looked a little spooked.

Willie explained, "I saw his car in the parking garage." Her eyes were amused.

But that only made Hillary wonder *when* Willie had "seen" that the car was there.

Angus urged, "You women sit down so we can."

Paul got up from the couch.

But Willie said, "Sit." Then she asked Hillary, "May I look around? I really need the 'feel' of Tate." She was being a little droll. She didn't want to sit down and have to look at Paul... yet.

"Of course." As Hillary gave permission, she noticed that Paul prevented Jim from joining him on the couch. Paul was maneuvering them all so that Willie would have to sit by him. Clever man, she thought.

Willie had continued explaining to Hillary, "I mean everything. Really nosy. Drawers and closets." She leaned down and picked up the friendly, welcoming cat.

Hillary was briefly conscious of the fact that the cat was a natural-born hostess. Or was it a "familiar"?

She replied, "No secrets," giving Willie full leave to poke into anything of Tate's.

As Willie turned away to scan the whole room—her glance passing right through Paul—she looked like a witch, one you wanted on your side. Hillary would have liked to just watch Willie, who was so fascinating, but Angus took Hillary's arm and deliberately moved to the couch. Paul prevented their sitting down with one straight, hard stare and an unwelcoming gesture for them to get away!

Angus had threatened to sit in Willie's preserved place to tease Paul. Hillary knew it had been deliberate because Angus then pulled up two of the dining-room chairs quite readily, and they sat there where Angus had planned they'd sit all along. Men!

Before Hillary sat next to Angus, she tried again to phone Carter. Then, since the guests knew the basics of Tate's disappearance, they began questioning. They took Hillary carefully over every detail. They each looked at the note and read it. They questioned Hillary about being called "Boy," and she told them about the Lambert children playing Tarzan and how she'd been too young to be anything but Tarzan's found child.

Then Paul asked for Carter's number. Hillary got the address book and showed it to him.

Paul nodded, then told her, "I'll find Carter." And he copied down the number.

"It's an unlisted number," Hillary warned.

"No problem."

Since more than an hour had passed, Hillary tried Carter's number yet again. There still was no answer.

After that, Angus told about the note to Beanpole on the refrigerator, and they all had a good laugh.

Then he mentioned the nostalgia tape for Boy, and
they listened to the first of that. It was obviously a
long tape, of remembered things that could be important; therefore, it needed to be studied for any hidden
meanings. So they put it aside until later, in order to
use their time together to question and discuss.

There was little that Hillary could add. She knew
nothing about Tate's job, other than the fact that she
was editor of the women's page and the types of articles that were used. Hillary listed her sister's degrees,
mentioned other positions she'd held, expounded on
her personality and her general habits.

But they were discussing a grown woman with a
sister who hadn't really lived with her since Tate was
eighteen and had left home to attend college. At that
time Hillary had been eight years old. While she and
her sisters saw one another several times during the
year, it was "visiting," and although they spoke fre-
quently on the phone, it was catchup stuff.

So the Lamberts were good, decent, and as close as
scattered families could be. They were educated, con-
scientious and law-abiding. All of it was just about
what the group of investigators had expected to hear.

Angus gave his theory that Tate had accidentally
dug out or seen something that was going to happen—or could be avoided; that she was simply being
held until it was completed and her information,
whatever it was, would be obsolete. He found the
others had come to the same conclusion. This Tate
lamb had gotten into some wolf's den quite by acci-
dent. That made it tough to figure out.

Willie quietly looked over everything, all through
the apartment, adding her own comments, touching
things. Poking around. She took the longest with that

silly fish, mounted and hung behind the sofa, and she smiled at it. To study the fish, she was standing in front of the couch, and she about had Paul on his ear. He was sitting almost in front of her, and he never took his eyes from her, but she ignored him. Was Willie really interested in the fish? Hillary wondered.

They were all aware of the tension between Willie and Paul. The other two men smiled at each other, enjoying the method Willie took to torture Paul.

But Hillary wondered if Willie wasn't genuinely studying the fish. "Seeing" with it. Maybe Willie could "see" Tate bragging about that fish, the first of legal size she'd ever caught. Who but Tate would have had it mounted? Who but Tate could have convinced someone to stuff and mount such a fish?

Hillary was suddenly overwhelmed with the helpless feeling of not being able to solve something important for a sister. It was appalling. She was a searcher, but not the right kind to help Tate.

Hillary became fractionally more silent in the easy conversational exchange in the room. She hadn't considered that every day, all of those present dealt with people and their emotions. They were aware of Hillary's distress almost as quickly as she.

Willie came to her just as Angus told her softly, "I got beer. I think there're some pretzels in the cupboard. Let's go see."

To strengthen that distraction, enunciating meticulously, Willie said, "I loathe beer. Do you have something else?"

Hillary heard one segment of her scattered thoughts bet that with Willie rejecting beer, it must be that Paul loved beer above all things. And her distraction was begun.

Just then Paul stood up. He took out a pad and pencil and held them in one hand as he said to Willie, "Come and sit down. You're making us all nervous. Give me the cat."

Willie listened as the cat mewed as if to apologize to Paul for not greeting him sooner. She sniffed his mouth and purred, then she rubbed her cheeks against his face to mark him as her territory. His laugh was a marvelous rumble. Willie figured the man and cat were soul mates. He murmured to the cat as he took Willie's arm and sat her down, then joined her on the "reserved" sofa. Willie pretended Paul had vanished, but the cat crawled up Paul's chest and sat on his shoulder, between the pair, purred in his ear and rubbed her chin in his hair. Willie saw that the cat was an outrageous flirt.

Angus paused at the kitchen counter to watch. He told Paul, "Name her and you've got yourself a cat."

"It might take a while to find the right name. Females need to be treated right." Paul's deep voice fit him, Hillary thought. But with his words, Willie gave him her first glance, which he captured and held as they exchanged a meaningful look.

Angus warned, "Don't you two make up yet. I need your full attention."

Paul smiled at Willie, and his eyes went as lazy as Jim's. That made the men all laugh. It was such a sexual look.

Willie turned away as if unimpressed, but her tongue sneaked out and quickly touched her lips.

As they had planned, all that byplay had given Hillary a breather, and she felt that she was back in control. Angus worked with her as they got out pretzels and made lemonade, then she asked, "How did you know Tate had pretzels?"

He replied, "I looked when I was making breakfast this morning."

Only *this* morning? she thought. She'd only known Angus one day? Incredible. Of course, Angus had known her for two days. But she'd been asleep that first, almost twenty-four hours.

When they carried the snacks into Tate's living room, their guests were still watching the cat with Paul. As the hosts sat down, Paul commanded of Willie, "Tell us anything you think." He was holding the pad and pencil.

She sipped the lemonade and licked her lips. She set the glass on the sofa table in front of her and then she said, "The names Beanpole and Boy are clues. I'll take the tape home and listen to it carefully. Tate wrote that note and left those messages just in case. She's hidden them so that if her captors should look, the clues will be meaningless. But if we can understand that, we'll have the key to the solution."

Paul said, "Angus, speaking of keys, if they have Tate, they probably have the key to this place. Hillary ought not to stay here."

"Right. When we made our first check, I didn't find a purse that was being used—that is, one with the usual contents. I should have been aware of the key as a part of it. That could have been a bad mistake. Thanks, Paul."

"Don't just remove Hillary. Take all her things." Paul clutched the pad and pencil so his words were conventional.

"We'll restore the apartment to the way we found it. Good point. She'll be with me."

Hillary said to Angus, "My key fits your lock. So Tate's key would fit your door."

"No one knows I know you."

Paul advised, "Take all precautions."

"Tate told me the security here is exceptional," Hillary offered.

"I didn't come through it," Paul replied.

"Neither did I," Jim said.

Willie told Hillary, "They are basically dishonest; they feel they've won when they get away with something like that. It's probably a sign of lingering immaturity." She gave the men a droll glance. "On the other hand, I came through security. Fortunately, Angus had cleared me."

Paul explained, "Security is for honest people and amateurs."

"Are you accusing me of being an amateur?" Willie cast Paul a haughty look.

"Not in some things," he growled softly.

Hillary questioned cautiously, "You two got in without checking in with security? You're making me very nervous."

"You'll be with me." Angus gave her a confident side look from under an arrogantly quirked brow that matched any arrogant expression of Paul's. "If Tate's captors take you, they'll get me, too. And that would be a big mistake." Then he inquired, "Okay. Now, Paul, what's going on that could fit this theory? You have your finger on the city's pulse. What's happening?"

Paul explained they had a wide choice. There was a fraud ring tottering on the brink of being revealed; the prosecutor needed only a witness. There was a suspected extortion and the possibility of a canary to sing all the notes. Then, too, there was a three-time murderer due to be executed, with the rumor he was really innocent of the fourth killing. And there was some hanky-panky among a candidate's coterie that might ensnare the candidate in a politically fatal mess.

"Want more?" Paul asked, doodling on his pad. "There is corruption suspected in one of the international businesses, and some of the stockholders have hired their own investigators. You'd, uh...throw up over the smell of the rot. And a star has been fingered as a kingpin in drug trafficking. The...is the hero of the single-numeral age group.

"These are rooted here in Chicago. These are the ones I know about. There're more. Each of these is close to toppling, but each could still be salvaged by the upper echelon with a bit more time or if they can find a patsy.

"These are all just the kind of thing about which Tate could have found some information, and these are all people who would hesitate at murdering a witness but would risk holding someone hostage anonymously until the release would be convenient. I've gathered this much since Angus called this morning. I've people on some of these. Jim, you can help with two. One's a beauty."

Jim gave Paul his lazy, laid-back smile and said, "I'd be delighted."

"It could be chancy."

"Fun."

Paul scowled. "Fun?"

Jim raised lazy brows and amended the word to "Interesting?"

"It could be deadly." Paul's voice was flat.

"Maybe I should take that one," Angus put in strongly.

Hillary protested, "No!" just as Paul's "No" made the decision. "Jim would be best at this one. Just pay attention, hero."

"Yes, sir." Jim slowly lifted his hand and gave a sloppy, curling salute.

Paul then told Angus, "The best way you can help is to keep Hillary safe. I'll charge you with that." Then he commanded Willie, "You check out that tape and let me know what you think. Any clues. Could you make a printed copy? It would help us all in going over the words."

Amazingly, Willie accepted his abrupt directions. "I can do that."

Paul gave Willie his approval: "I also think Tate was planting clues."

Willie agreed. "A dull, taped voice is out of character for her. She made her voice that way so that anyone else would give up listening. It would seem a nostalgia tape. The note was to tip you off, Hillary."

"I've never done this kind of hunting, so I just thought Tate was being sentimental," Hillary said.

"You're too worried about her to pay attention. To us it was obvious. We'll find what she's trying to make you see."

"I don't quite know how to thank you all for helping. Whatever your fees, our family will meet them."

"We do this for fun—interest." Jim changed the word with a slow, humorous look at Paul.

Paul stood up and dropped the cat down on the sofa but smoothed her fur in apology. He asked Angus, "Need help getting Hillary's stuff out of here?"

"We'll manage," Angus replied. "She just has the one case."

Paul dismissed Angus and the others by turning to Willie. Still holding his pad and pencil, he said carefully, "I'll see you home."

Rather airily she replied, "I have my car, and I need to get to the tape."

"I need a half hour to talk to you."

She smiled. "Perhaps another time."

"Come on." He ignored her dismissal and took her arm.

"You want me to sit on your shoulder and purr," she guessed.

"Something like that."

The spectators didn't hear any more, because Paul had taken Willie out the door and closed it.

Jim said, "I feel we're being deserted. It's still early. I probably should catch up with Paul and Willie and get the tape. Farewell, you two. And I mean just that."

Hillary watched after Jim, astonished to see how quickly he could move. She said to Angus, "He wasn't drugged!"

"Who?"

"Jim."

"Of course not. They've all got all their brain cells, and we'll be giving those cells one hell of a workout. We've got a lot to do. Let's get out of here."

"Yes."

"It could be dangerous. If it's something that big that could be toppled, the snatchers might change their minds about murder, and those murdered could be not only Tate but us. People do desperate, despicable things when their own hides are in danger."

"I know," Hillary said faintly.

"Stay at my place."

"Please."

"Please," he amended very seriously.

"No, I was asking if I may."

"You may."

Since Hillary had bathed at Tate's, the towels from the bath were taken to his place and put in his washer-dryer. Back at Tate's, she and Angus went through everything. He even monitored what was in the garbage.

They washed up the dishes and carefully put them away, and they dusted surfaces. All of Hillary's clothing was removed, and Tate's things, which had been pushed aside, were carefully replaced. Angus and Hillary went over everything and discussed what might have been disturbed. The address book was returned to the drawer. "I need to call Tate's friends," she said.

"It's too late tonight. Do that tomorrow."

They went over the whole apartment, discussing whether it was the same. Then they carried away the excess—or new—garbage and replaced the eggs they'd taken from the refrigerator for breakfast. They replaced the pretzel box, which now held only a few.

Back in Angus's apartment, they took the towels out of the dryer, and he carried them back so Hillary could hang them exactly as they'd been before.

As they returned to his place, Angus told her, "You have to know this is a complicated case."

"Yes."

"We'll solve it."

"I hope so." She went into his apartment and automatically took off her shoes.

"You might as well put your things away in the bedroom. You'll probably be here awhile."

"I do hope this doesn't inconvenience you, but if I had to stay someplace else I would go crazy wondering what was happening. You're very kind to allow me to stay here."

"I'm all heart."

"You really are a very nice man."

They were in the bedroom by then, and as Hillary began to unpack her things she found that all the red wispy nothings were gone from his drawer. She smiled secretly and wondered what had happened to those feminine things. And there were empty hangers in his closet where feminine clothing had hung. She didn't mention the missing items but simply hung her own things away.

Angus moved cautiously. She was back in his bedroom. Where would she sleep? In his bed? Not making any sudden moves, he took off his shirt and shoes, took clean pajamas from the drawer and with calculated casualness said, "You can use the bath first. You have to put your things in there anyway."

She went ahead, and after a time she emerged from the bath in her oversize T-shirt, which more than adequately covered her panties. She finished putting her things away while he was in the bathroom, and he came out to fit her empty case into the top of his closet.

He was excessively aware they were in the bedroom together, and he was careful to appear natural so that he wouldn't bring this fact to her attention. His entire

body waited breathlessly to see what would happen.
Then she went over and got into the far side of the
bed!

She said, "Angus, how could I have been so lucky
to have stumbled onto you?"

"You Lambert women seem prone to do that,
stumbling into trouble."

She inquired with a small smile, "Are you trouble,
too?"

"Well, I should hope so!"

"I feel safe with you."

He was appalled. She felt safe? With a starving sex
advocate?

He heard that she was saying, "I couldn't believe
that you would let Paul take over and run the meeting
and direct who did what."

He had to blink a couple of times to get his brain
into gear. "Uh. Why not? He knows what he's
doing." He sat on the bed and every second he
expected her to question his right to be there.

"What does Paul do...really?"

He was distracted from the exact weightiness of
what she asked, since he was lifting the covers and
getting into bed with her, so he barreled right into it,
replying right off the bat: "He's a cop—" Awareness
as to exactly what he was saying hit him then, but his
tongue stumbled on: "A special investigator." He
hurried faster. "An old and trusted friend who happens to work in the police department. Hillary, I *had*
to call him. Time is of the essence in this. We're fight-
ing all sorts of very delicate odds. All three of the
people here tonight will help us. They'll be coming
back again," he assured her as he lay there petrified,

expecting her to explode in several kinds of indignation. Since she was still silent, he went on talking in order to distract her. "If the snatchers 'win' whatever criminal thing is being done, they might not be able to allow Tate to live, so we have that facing us. They might not want a witness. And if they 'lose' whatever it is, a witness might be a nasty burden to them. We'll have to be very careful. We have to all stay alive and, while working full tilt, still be very, very careful."

"Yes."

He had to ask, "Are you angry with me?"

"Of course not. Why should I be angry with you?"

He told it all. "I called Paul as soon as I got back to my apartment after breakfast."

"I realize that."

"You told me not to."

"I'm glad you did."

"Hillary Lambert, you're a woman after my own heart."

Suddenly she asked, "Do you realize we're in the same bed?"

He thought: Here it comes. He took a breath to be ready to placate....

She went on, "I'm sorry. I just realized it. I should be on the sofa. It just seemed so natural that I— I am sorry. I didn't mean to embarrass you."

He hurried to assure her. "Uh...I'm not embarrassed. It's perfectly all right. We did sleep together last night, and you *did* behave. I feel *safe* with you, so you can stay."

She laughed! "Well, the cat can chapero— Where's the cat? The cat's not here! Do you remember seeing it in Tate's apartment? Where is it?"

Of all things he'd expected to upset her, he'd never thought once about the damned cat.

Five

Hillary flipped back the sheet and got out of bed as Angus said, "I'll go."

"No, I took her down there, so I'm really responsible." She retrieved her shorts and pulled them on so that they disappeared under the outsize T-shirt. "And I want to get Tate's address book. I need to start calling her friends. I just can't risk having it there and having somebody take it. I'd never find the numbers, and I must call them."

"What would they know?"

"I'm not sure. I just feel I should tell them I'm here. Tate obviously talked to Carter about whatever was happening. She might have said something to the others."

"That could be," he admitted.

She took Tate's key from her purse. They went to the front door, and, allowing her toes to get themselves into her shoes, she said, "I'll be right back."

"Hold it just a minute."

On some unknown impulse, Angus returned to the bedroom to take his gun from its hiding place—a sliding panel at the back side of his dresser. The cubbyhole made that top drawer a little short. He checked the gun out, and it worked slickly.

Still barefoot and wearing only pajama bottoms, he went soundlessly to the opened door and found her gone. He became sharply alert to possible danger to her. He stepped out into the hall. The dimmed nightlights along the base of the wall were on, so it was a little eerie out there.

Because the halls followed the bend of the structure, there was a hundred-thirty-degree curve between the doors of the apartments. Farther down the hall, Angus saw a man in dark clothes who seemed to materialize in the hallway out of a murky mist, moving, but making not a whisper of sound.

Angus tensed to advance but heard Tate's door click open as the man came closer. Angus's muscles went rigid, and he became fully alert and ready for action. The man carried no obvious weapon. Angus saw a portion of Hillary behind the slight bend of wall as, unaware, she turned back to test that Tate's door was locked. When she came away from the door, toward him, he heard her gasp.

In a low hissing voice the man asked her, "Why'd you wanta see Frank Carter?"

The man's words were difficult for Hillary to understand. "Who?" She clutched the cat and the address book to her chest and stood straight and protective.

"At the hospital—"

But Angus had drifted from his door like a patch of fog. He said softly, "Freeze." His word was like a cold wind that carried a quick chill the length of the hall and stopped the man's explanation dead on his tongue.

The bulky man by Hillary shifted with a small jerk, but he held his hands free of his body in the ancient gesture of a noncombatant. His voice was hushed and a little offended. Indignant. "What? Who're you?"

Hillary gasped to see the gun in Angus's hands, and she stood frozen, not knowing what was expected of her.

Angus replied to the bulk, "I'm her escort. Don't move. Honey, come behind me."

As she moved to obey, the bulk's response came rather plaintively, "I just wanta know why the lady wanted Frank, that's all."

"We weren't looking for that particular Carter. We're searching for another one whose first name—or last name—we don't know."

The man chided, "That's a mean gun. You got a license?"

Angus countered, "You got a badge?"

The man laughed without a sound. "My 'badge' wouldn't pass muster."

Angus replied, "My gun would."

"Yeah. I see it. You don't want Frank?"

"Not for a minute."

"No problem. Okay?"

Angus pushed: "How did you get in past security?"

"Same as them others. Same way as your friends come in."

"I see. You may go. But leave down the stairs." That would take him past the security desk, where he wasn't registered, Angus knew.

The stranger complained, "Ah, naw, don't do that to me."

"Let me see your driver's license."

There was a toothy grin. "Which one?"

"The real one."

Moving a little elaborately, he inquired, "Ya trust me?"

"Why not?"

The laugh was puffs of harsh air that revealed genuine amusement. "Here. I'd have been here at a decent time, but you had company. I'm harmless."

What an interesting word for that bulk to know, Angus mused. "Ever work gumshoe?"

"Yeah. All the time."

"I might contact you."

"Use this number. Ask for Finnig."

Hillary's eyes had adjusted to the faint light, and she could see that Finnig was in his late thirties and not bad looking. A big, rough man. His bulk was mostly in his shoulders. He was intimidating.

Angus found Finnig wasn't the name on the "real" license, and it was Angus's turn to grin.

"Well," Finnig explained, "a guy can't be too careful."

"What's the battered Frank Carter do?"

"He's not gonna be doing anything for a while. We just wanted to be sure he'd been, uh, marked paid up in full."

"I can see how he'd feel that way."

Hillary had to concentrate to fill in the missing letters in Finnig's words. She whispered to Angus, "Was Frank the one in the coma?"

But with a "Yeah," it was Finnig who agreed.

"Why was that woman so rude?" Hillary was still a little huffy.

Finnig explained, "She's scared."

"Why don't they go to the police?" Hillary wanted to know.

That left Finnig almost helpless with amusement. When he could speak, he said, "Police are for the good guys."

She couldn't leave it. "Aren't you a good guy?"

"To me, I am." But Finnig was restless and added, "I like visiting, but it's time for them to check the halls, you understand."

Angus said, "Don't come back; I'm going to tell them to stagger their checks so you don't know when it's safe."

"Smart. So long."

The couple stood and watched as he appeared to float away on lighted, busy feet. He didn't take the stairs that led to the entrance.

"Get inside." Angus clicked something on the gun and handed it to her before he vanished.

Clutching the gun, the cat and the address book, Hillary slipped through Angus's door and finally let the cat go. Inside, she leaned against the locked door and listened, hearing nothing for a long time. A gun. A snakelike weapon there in his hand. Now in hers. She looked at it in horror. Angus had been ready to use it. Could this whole thing really be as bad as Angus had tried to tell her it was?

He didn't have a key, so he scratched on his door and spoke his name softly against the panel. She only opened the door the width of the chain. He said, "Let me in."

She closed the door to release the chain, then opened it to him. He came in, took the gun from her and leaned down to kiss her mouth in a quick...what? Greeting? Reassurance? *Possession.*

The cat wound around them, purring, which reminded Angus to go fetch back the litter box. After he returned and when the cat realized they were moving toward the bedroom, it went ahead and jumped up on the bed. The cat was wide-awake, mewing inquiringly and wanting to visit.

But they were silent. Hillary went around to her side of the bed and slipped under the sheet. She sat, watching, as Angus hunted in a drawer for a holster, slid the gun into it and hung it on the bedpost. Hillary stayed wide-eyed. She was shocked that Angus handled the gun and placed it as naturally as someone would, say, an ashtray, for convenience.

Hillary eyed him. "People may hide children, but they are rarely dangerous to searchers." She asked softly, "What do maritime investigators really do?"

"They are prepared for any eventuality. People can be very sudden where money or fraud or manipulation is involved and they are about to be caught in the act."

"What made you take the gun into the hall?" She was a little stimulated and felt chatty.

"A hunch." Until then, even with Finnig, his voice had been reasonable and mild. Now it became steely. "If you *ever* again go out into the hall before I tell you to, I'm liable to throttle you. Do you understand me plainly?''

"Yes." That wasn't an unreasonable request, and she realized she'd been stupid, so she tried to placate him. "It was only a couple of doors down."

"That's all it takes, and—''

"And this place has the best security of any of the apartment complexes I've ever seen."

He dismissed her defense. "You had just been with four people, three of whom came into the building without checking in with security."

"Three?"

"Paul, Jim and Finnig."

"Yes. How'd they do that?" She snatched at the red herring.

And he followed it. "There's an empty apartment just above the overhang on the lake. They shinnied up a post and got in an unlocked window. I told security about it and can hardly wait for tonight when Paul and Jim try to come in that way."

She laughed, relaxing.

But he wasn't deterred after all, because his voice again was steel as he told her, "And if I ever tell you to do anything, you are to obey me without question. Do you hear me?"

"I understand."

"That isn't good enough. I want your solemn promise."

"I promise."

He took a deep breath, and his hand trembled for the first time since the unexpectedly harmless episode began. "You scared the bloody hell out of me. I told you to wait."

"I am sorry."

"You could have been snatched just like Tate."

"Why would they want me?"

"We're looking for her," he reminded Hillary.

"How could anyone know that?"

"Finnig could have been one, checking you out. He might not even know Frank. Only that we were inquiring about him."

Her sound was rather small: "Oh."

"Yes. 'Oh.' Pay attention. Now do you understand why you have to listen to me? Obey me?"

"I will. I promise."

"Get to sleep," he said.

"You don't mind if I sleep here?"

"Just stay on your own side. Cross the center line and you're in real trouble." He didn't sound inviting at all.

"Okay."

He turned off the light.

Having been wakened and moved from one apartment back to this one, the cat wasn't as sleepy and began to lick its pristine fur. In the silence, its licking was very audible. The two people listened to the cat working away, but they were really only conscious of each other.

He felt he'd been a little harsh with her. He ought not to say anything more. They were there in his bed, together, and he wasn't sure that if they started talking, he could control himself and not try to be...manipulative.

There she was, lying on the other side of the center line, across the wide expanse of his bed, just at the tip of his fingers if he stretched out his arm. There she was with her naked body encased in discardable T-shirt and panties. Close by. He'd better think of something else. Finnig.

Angus got up and wrote down the number Finnig had given him. He'd have Paul check it out. A contact shouldn't ever be ignored. He came back to bed and lay down with an impatient sigh.

"Are you hungry?" she asked.

Well, yes, he was, now that she mentioned it, but she meant food. "Yeah." He threw back the sheet and stood up.

Hillary and the cat left the bed with eagerness. Neither was sleepy. Hillary wanted to talk about their encounter with that man. It had been out of a novel! Those things never happened. Yes, they did. She stopped off in the living room at the desk and again tried Carter's number. Even at that hour there was no answer.

Not saying anything, the two adults and the little cat went into the kitchen and Angus turned on the light. Hillary watched as he put slices of Mary Jane's *perfect* bread into the toaster and got out butter, sugar and cinnamon. He set a pan on the stove and poured in milk, then got down some cocoa.

The cat inquired about a bite for itself, and Angus gave it some ice cream. Hillary didn't comment on his feeding that innocent cat something so unsuitable.

She judged Angus's mood. He was a little touchy for some reason. Surely he wasn't still grouchy because she didn't wait for him to go to Tate's. The incident in the hall was interesting, but if Angus hadn't been so tense, it wouldn't have been extraordinary.

To hear that chilling "Freeze!" and see a bare-chested, pajama-bottomed, barefoot Angus in such a dangerously serious stance had been startling, to say the least. Where did any citizen see such a serious threat—other than on TV?

The man in the hall had meant her no harm. He'd needed to ask her a question. That was all. Angus had overreacted. Of course, she'd been a little surprised by the man, for she hadn't expected anyone to seek her out in a strange town. But the man, Finnig, was obviously harmless. The wonder of it was that he hadn't panicked and fled. Then Angus probably would have shot him. After such an act, there would have been all sorts of complications, and living with Angus this way, she would have had to stand by him.

She looked at him. He was a marvelous man. Beautifully made. His eyes were so green. And he was sweet. He took up for a cat's rights. And he had meant to protect her. He'd trembled when it was over. While he handled the gun with great familiarity, he'd probably never actually *aimed* it at anyone, and the reality of it had probably rattled him. He was such a gentle man....

Angus glanced at Hillary while he stirred the milk. Her smile was faint and mushy, while her eyes softened so that she looked like a pushover. He knew she was impressed with how he'd handled himself out there in the hall with that hood. So she must realize what a stupid thing she'd done, going out without him to protect her. She didn't know how to apologize, but he could tell she was sorry. She was feeling the female reaction to the dominant male. She'd probably insist on rewarding him. He smiled back just a little cockily.

Women were all the same. He could read them and predict them just like that. He didn't actually snap his fingers; she might jump on his body—now—just when the cocoa needed stirring into the milk. He didn't want her to just give in. He wanted her to make him work a little bit first. Women who just lay down and rolled over the first chance they had were boring. *Almost* boring. No real challenge. There were times that a man liked to feel he'd "won" the woman.

He straightened so she could admire his good, strong body. He was glad he was hairy and that he didn't have to blush for lack of muscles. He didn't resist moving around just a tad, for her sake.

Finnig was a bad one. The way he'd reacted hadn't been that of a decent citizen. He might just as well have worn a sign. How many times had the man been under a deadly gun? Finnig hadn't even cringed. Whatever he was involved with, it included a serious use of guns.

Angus relished the fact that he'd snared a phone number from Finnig. All he had done was to pretend not to be quite on the line about his gun. The number might be a phony. Paul could find out.

So that she wouldn't become depressed with her stupidity and the fact that she'd so carelessly risked his life, he gave Hillary a glance for her morale, and she returned it with such a tender smile. In anticipation, his body tingled down its length. Tonight. He allowed his eyes to be boldly personal as he enjoyed the sight of her.

She had a great body. Her skin was nice. Women had such smooth bodies. They were so sweet to touch. Like satin, she was. He knew because she'd crossed the center line last night.

Why hadn't she thanked him for saving her neck tonight? He'd given her all this time to be ashamed of her rash behavior and to be grateful to him. God knew where she'd be now—or in what condition—if he hadn't gotten there with his gun and stopped Finnig.

But she hadn't said a word. She just sat there with that soft look. She was probably ready to make up for putting them in such danger. Did she expect him to make the first move? He supposed he could. He let his smile become visible. Such a lot of work. But my, oh my, she would be worth it.

Reality intruded. What if she was so indiscreet that she was unhealthy? She'd made no protest or token hesitation about sleeping in his bed tonight. She looked like a newborn woman; she looked so clean and pure. How did a guy ask? "Uh . . . Hillary . . ."

"Mmm?" She raised her brows in polite inquiry.

"Is there any . . . reason . . . we shouldn't . . . uh . . . use the same toothbrush?" Holy Moses, why had he ever said "toothbrush"? Idiotic.

She replied quickly, "I have my own." She smiled again in order to reassure him that she wouldn't ask to use his toothbrush. The dear man! How sheltered he lived. All alone in a big city. So isolated. To worry about sharing a toothbrush! He was probably inexperienced, too. Then she wondered if he worried about sharing the sheets. That caused her to frown a little.

He assumed, in turn, that she was wondering if he was diseased. So he assured her, "No problem."

That comment puzzled Hillary. He'd asked if she wanted to use his toothbrush, she assured him she had her own, and he said "No problem." Had he *wanted* to share his toothbrush? Was this some kinky kind of fetish?

In watching her face for a blush of guilt or some clue, Angus ignored the cocoa and it boiled over. That was distracting, and they made a flurry of activity in cleaning it up. What was left was drinkable. Fortunately, unlike Angus, the toaster was automatic, so the toast wasn't burned, but Hillary was the one who buttered it and sprinkled it with cinnamon and sugar.

They munched and sipped in silence. Angus knew she was girding herself up to placate him, so he would occasionally catch her eye and smile a little to encourage her.

She smiled back, and finally she said, "You must have scared Mr. Finnig out of ten years' growth with that gun. Whatever made you do that?"

He was stunned. She wasn't chagrined; she was stupid! She had no intention of apologizing. What a dumb woman. "He is a very dangerous man," Angus said in a slow, dangerous way.

"Don't be such a silly—"

He went rigid with indignation.

"—man. Angus, he just wanted to know why we wanted that particular Carter."

"And if you'd said he wasn't the one you wanted...and Finnig hadn't believed you and had taken you back into Tate's apartment to ask you another time or two?"

"You watch too much TV."

His blood pressure elevated. Very carefully choosing his words, he mentioned, "There's nothing worse than naive country bumpkins in the wicked, wicked big city."

"Kansas City is no hole-in-the-wall." She gave him a cool look.

"No one compares Kansas City to Chicago."

"We've had our share of criminals," she said in defense of Kansas City's darker side.

"Amateurs."

"They do the exact same thing."

"There isn't any comparison at all." His words came down hard on the difference between the cities.

"So I'm supposed to suspect every single person I meet in Chicago?"

"It wouldn't hurt to be cautious."

"With you?"

"I'm different. You can trust me."

"One out of how many millions? I got into the wrong apartment, so I'm supposed to trust you, but a man in the hall—*on whom you hold a gun*—is open to suspicion? I'm not sure I follow your reasoning, Mr. Behr."

Probably not tonight, he thought.

"Hillary, you're a big girl. You travel. You've seen people—you know how their minds work. You've seen all the nastiness between people, the trickery, the slyness, and you can sit there and be that accepting of a strange man, in a strange hall at an odd hour, who has searched you out?"

"He was protecting his boss."

"Try it the other way."

She frowned. "His boss was protecting him? Finnig is the boss?"

"That Frank Carter took the beating for Finnig."

"Now, why would you think that?"

"Didn't you hear him? He said he wanted to be sure he was paid off in full. Whoever beat that Carter was paying Finnig back for a beating."

"Surely not."

"Goldilocks, you're such an innocent, you scare the hell out of me. Who let you loose in this world? I'm terrified by the thought of you wandering around, looking for people and managing to get through. How close have you been to disaster—how many times?"

She could recall a time or two. She said, "Basically, people are honest."

"You're surviving on borrowed time. If you were a cat, you'd be on life fifteen."

She was getting a little huffy. "You exaggerate."

"Not if your conduct tonight was any example of how you operate."

"He scared me—"

"I'm glad to hear that."

"—a little, and if he'd been threatening, I'd have thrown the cat on him and bolted, screaming bloody murder."

"You always carry a handy cat for emergencies?"

"You're being nasty," she said.

"I'm trying to get it through your thick skull—" not tonight "—that you're mind-bogglingly careless. You need some training in self-preservation."

"I know judo." She gave him a diminishing look.

She didn't fit the mold. He gave her a disgruntled look back. She was a female reject. How had God allowed this flawed woman to get loose? She was the kind of woman who ruined men. She'd stupidly get into trouble and then some good man would get killed trying to protect her. She was a burden to the world.

She was so damned good-looking and sweet that she lured men into doing all sorts of things for her, like going out into a dark hall in just pajama bottoms and a gun to save her damned skin. No practical brains at all. A disaster.

He looked at her with sour regard. A man would find himself doing all sorts of things to please a woman like her. Carrying, fetching—looking at her and plotting ways to get her into his bed. Damn. It sure as hell wouldn't be that night.

How many men had come home from the office and found women in their beds? The perfect movie plot. Any other man would have had her then. Any other man would have stripped, gotten into bed with her, said, "Well, hel-lo there!" and gotten on with it. What had he done? Waited. Given her water to drink. And waited. He was still waiting.

Why wasn't she flirting with him? Why hadn't she giggled and rolled her eyes at him over sharing his bed? Either she was so jaded that it was no big deal to share a bed with a stranger, or she was such an innocent that she didn't realize her virtue was in danger. She hadn't really paid any attention to the fact that she was in his apartment and would be sharing his bed. She'd acted just as if they were buddies at scout camp! Here she was, a ripe woman, and here he was, a ready man, and . . . zero.

It could have been such a great adventure. Just like in the books. A chance encounter, a beautiful, admiring woman, no preliminaries, instant passion fulfilled.... Yeah, sure. She didn't know the rules. Or she knew too many. She hadn't read the script.

"Let's go to bed," he said. What a great beginning! Now she was supposed to say "Oh, darling!" or "This is so sudden!" It would be a little sudden. He ought to wait another day or so.

She chatted. "I'm really worn out. This has been a long, exhausting day. I surely appreciate all you've done to help. The time. Thank you so much."

She held out her hand. That's what she did.

He shook it.

Then he followed her into the bedroom and watched her go around the bed to her side. She hadn't been there even forty-eight hours and she already owned a side of his bed. He'd charge her rent. He smiled. Not necessarily in the coin of the realm.

And a remarkable thing happened. She said, "It's a little cool in here, don't you think? Do you have another blanket?"

"No," he lied. "I've only been here two months. I haven't accumulated winter stuff yet." Then he added pithily, "I'll adjust the air conditioner."

"Oh, no. If it isn't cold for you, I can put a folded sheet on my side, and it'll probably be enough."

"I'll change it. I'm cool, too." Yeah. Cool. Sure. He could set a fire, he was so hot. He went to the thermostat and clicked it several times—setting it considerably colder. He wondered if his canine teeth had sharpened and his ears had gotten fuzzy. He rubbed his face, but it hadn't gotten wolfishly hairy. His smile was wicked.

They got into each side of that overly large bed. She said, "Good night."

He replied, "Good night, Little Red Riding Hood."

"I thought it was Goldilocks," she murmured as she yawned.

"You're wandering in the woods, Little Red Riding Hood."

"I've told you, people are nicer than you believe. Look at you. Here I am, and look how you've helped me. You have the kindest heart. Your parents would be proud of you."

Proud? His mother would be shocked.

He turned out the light and frowned at Hillary resentfully. Why did she have to bring up his parents?

What a nasty thing to do to a man bent on seduction! He leaned across the center line and kissed her rather roughly. Then he growled, "Sleep warm."

"Thank you, Angus."

She didn't have to be so nice about it. That wasn't the kind of kiss he wanted to give her. He wanted to kiss her— It wasn't a good idea right now to think about the kind of kisses he wanted to give to Hillary Lambert.

The Lamb part of her name was appropriate. She was a strayed lamb and she was in his bed. He sent a wicked, slit-eyed look her way. Aloud he said, "Be sure to stay on your side of the center line, Little Red Riding Hood. You come over here, and you lose your sanctuary."

"I'll behave."

Yeah. That was the trouble.

How long would it take the air conditioner to make it cold enough in the room for her to come over the center line? He went to sleep waiting.

When she shivered and moved toward him, he was surprised to find her crowding him. He was on her side of the bed. He moved with calculation, and she gradually followed his heat. When he had her across the center line, he led her a little farther. *Then* he growled a wolfish "You're on my side of the bed."

"I'm freezing," she breathed groggily.

"Oh. Maybe I turned the thermostat the wrong way."

"I'm really cold."

"I can warm you nicely." And with some glee he took her into his arms and kissed her. His lips pulled at hers as he plastered her soft, cooled body to his hot flesh, and his hard, eager hands molded her shape to be sure she was real. He deepened the kiss, his breath roughening, and he knew it would happen tonight after all. He pulled her into his body's eager surface.

She kissed him back drowsily and slid her arms to hold him, too. Then she blew everything by murmuring, "How kind you are. I needed so badly to be held. I'm so worried about Tate."

Her words threw him clear off balance. He didn't lose the desire to make love to her—it ran almost beyond his control—but she wanted only support? She was grateful to be comforted because she worried about that sister who was probably just as careless about her safety as Hillary! Same mold. No wonder Hillary worried. And that was why she was there in his arms—to be comforted. Well, damn.

She then proceeded to go back to sleep! With him backed clear over on the edge of the bed and almost beyond the edge of his sanity, did she worry about him? About his needs? He could use a little comforting. Did she care about that? No, she went to *sleep*! Just as if everything were perfectly all right.

He carefully, gradually released her, got out of bed, reset the thermostat, went to the bathroom, came back and stood looking down at her. She was gorgeous. Mind-bending. She was driving him crazy. He'd never survive the night. He faced that. It was true. He was going to die of frustration. They'd find his half-clothed body, and she would go on trial for murdering him—and some damned judge would get her off. Even the prosecutor would be on her side. Angus put his hands into his hair, then dropped them in hopeless resignation.

No man should be put through the wringer this way. He'd go amok, just like the sex-crazed elephants who ran wild and uncontrollable during breeding time in India. What was a man to do? He went around and got into "her" side of his bed, and he took a long time getting to sleep. She slept like a *rock*. Just as if she had a clear conscience. Men had it tough. Women ruled. Men needed to get things back under their control.

Six

"Your breakfast is ready." The sentence floated around in Angus's head, and he frowned as he tried to figure out where he was and whose delicious voice was telling him that. If a female voice was fixing him breakfast, had someone stayed over? Who? If someone with a voice like that had stayed over, wouldn't his body be nice and contented? It wasn't. It felt like a firecracker that had been lit and smothered any number of insane, torturing times. He opened his eyes.

And there she was. Hillary Lambert, in person.

She was smiling just a little, in such a *kind* way that it irritated the liver out of him. How could she look that way when he'd had such a hell of a night? He stared back in a stony way. Let her carry the conversational ball.

She watched him with that same look. That same smile.

Disgruntled, he realized that he'd survived the night. That had to be a miracle. He was from hardy pioneer stock. That was the only answer to his survival under such duress. In such conditions. Sleeping in the same bed with a goddess who was too dumb to do anything about helping a poor mortal man survive.

Since she didn't say anything else, he snarled in a mean voice, "You survived crossing the center line last night." It was then that he found he was back on his own side of the bed.

"I was freezing."

Her voice was like a gentle, healing breeze. How did she do that? Sourly he asked, "Is that all you remember? That you were freezing?"

"You kissed me."

Her smile would have melted steel, but he wasn't affected. "Yeah."

She said softly, "So sweetly."

Sweetly! *Sweetly.* Sweetly? That had been his best shot. His full, stops-out, devastatingly sexual, skull-cracking best! And *she* thought it was..."sweet." She was a man killer. Not only that, but when he'd saved her hide from Finnig, she'd thought he'd "over-reacted." She had thought that. There was no way he was ever going to impress this woman. He would only be torn apart, ego busted, wrecked. The best thing to do was give up. There were mountains that finally defeated mortal man. She was one.

He rolled over so that he faced away from her, ignoring her.

She sat down on the edge of the bed and began to massage the muscles of his shoulders where they met his nape. His body was iron hard with stored tension.

She began to knead his back, and he groaned with the tortured pleasure as his body responded to her touch.

She nudged him flat onto his stomach and moved to kneel beside him to work his back. He allowed it. After a couple of minutes she said, "Do you want to shower first, or shall I bring your breakfast here? I can use the breadboard as a tray."

That sounded nice. He would permit it. "Here." He pointed to the bed.

She piled the pillows against the headboard on his side and crawled off the big bed.

He lay there, sulking, but willing now to be coaxed into a good humor. In a little while he heard her coming and moved slowly, as if he granted her his cooperation. He sat up, leaned against the plumped pillows and draped the sheet over his susceptible lap.

The tray of food smelled delicious. He looked at it with a carefully skeptical expression, as if he might still turn it down. The cat came up to see what was going on, and Hillary lifted it into her arms and stood there watching him. He gave her a cool glance. She was still wearing that kind smile.

He snubbed her and didn't speak or comment on the "tray." She'd made eggs Benedict for him. The coffee was perfect. She probably measured exactly. It was delicious. He ate in miffed silence that was beginning to embarrass him horribly. How could he act like such a juvenile? She didn't owe him one thing. Just because he was frustrated mindless, it wasn't her fault. She might not even realize she was a goddess. "Do you realize you're a goddess?" he asked in a grouchy voice.

"I thought I was Little Red Riding Hood in the woods."

See? She learned things only one at a time, then waited to grasp the next thing. He sighed. What a chore to have to teach her everything in progression from zilch up. He glanced up at her impatiently.

There she was, wearing that kind smile.

Was she amused by his asinine behavior? Tolerant? Did she think she was humoring him?

She said, "Carter still doesn't answer, but I managed to catch one of Tate's friends at home." Her voice saddened. "She asked, where is Tate?"

"Did you call them all?"

"I just got a couple of answering machines. Should I call Willie?"

"If there's anything on that tape at all that we need to know, she'd call, no matter what the hour. What are you doing up so bright and early?"

"We overslept."

He looked at the clock. "Ten-thirty?"

"You were very tired. I tried to waken you when the alarm went off, but you were dead to the world."

He understood that. He wasn't supposed to have survived the night. Not only had her being here killed him off, but she probably had the power to revive him, too. He could just imagine going through life with the woman, her killing him off every night and reawakening him every morning. Hell. Yep. Hell on earth. What sins had he ever committed that he—

"Shouldn't you call your office?" she asked.

"Yeah."

She took the phone from the bedside table and put it by his elbow. Then she took the cleared tray and went out of the room.

She was wearing jeans. They fit her sassy derriere exactly. Such a bottom should be against the law. She

walked out and any unknowing man would want to
follow...to his grief.

He called his secretary, and she asked, "Some
complications?"

He said, "Yeah."

"You have only one call. I've fielded the others."

"Good. Who?"

"He just said, 'Tell him Paul.'"

"Thanks." Then he hung up, rubbed his scratchy
cheek and yawned before he called Paul, left a message and again laid the receiver in its cradle.

He put the phone back on the table and sat there,
feeling rather tolerant. Was the way to a man's heart
really through his stomach? She'd fed him nicely and
now he was mellow? Not all of him.

As he was deciding to get up and get his day started,
Hillary came back into his room and over to the bed.
He simply watched her, giving her no clue how he felt.
She sat down next to him and asked, "Which crisis do
you think Tate stumbled into?"

"Which one?"

"Well, you know, the politician or the corporation
or that murderer?"

"We'll have to wait and see. I suppose it might be
one of them."

"So." She smiled a little. "What shall I do now?
You're the expert."

"Actually, I'm not," he admitted. "I'm extraordinary in admiralty law, maritime insurance and investigations when things like that go wrong. The experts
in this situation are those who came to Tate's apartment last night. We should wait to hear from Paul. He
called my office this morning, but I can't get him on
the phone. I left a message. No matter how the day

goes, the experts will all be here tonight. Since Paul
called the office and not here, it's probably just information. I'll tell him about Finnig's little visit. That'll
fascinate him, and it'll make Willie twitch. She'll go
over that tape again with new ears.''

Hillary had the audacity to reach over and push
back his hair. Just like that. With no outward sign, his
body went rigid from shock, and he was glad for the
concealing sheet. The contact of her fingers was like
being touched by an exotic being from another world
and not actually dying. He was certainly a survivor.
He'd never really realized that until today. He probably could even survive making love to a goddess.

She said, "Do you want to go back to sleep? Apparently we aren't to leave the apartment until we hear
from Paul. The pool is lovely; there's no one in it. We
could go swim.''

He'd forgotten the pool as a release for pent-up
tension. He nodded. But he didn't move. He was
mesmerized by her hand on his hair. Then she did a
terrible thing: she took her hand away.

He automatically reached out, took her hand and
put it back where it belonged.

She smiled at him, her eyes tender and her smile
sweet. Her lashes lowered as she looked down his
body, and since she blushed, he knew she hadn't in-
tended to do that. So. She was curious about him?

He reached out his hands, took hold of her under
her arms and drew her to him. She didn't object, so his
arms went around her and he squashed her against
him and bent his head to kiss her until she couldn't
think straight. She gasped and breathed oddly and
squirmed and squeaked and—helped. Yes, she did.
She really did!

So he just pulled her right on over across him and laid her right down on the other side, right on the bed's center line, and never quit kissing her any time along the way.

She ended up draped over him with the backs of her thighs over his hip and her feet on the other side. She was helpless. She didn't struggle. She had her arms wrapped around his head, and she was panting and twitching and driving him wild. Having driven him crazy wasn't really anything for her to brag about, because he'd already been almost there all night.

But she went berserk! They got her out of her clothes, and she rubbed her body against his chest and wiggled around, and she kissed him so that his mind was swamped with a purple haze of passion. His sight was distorted, his mouth hungry. His hands scrubbed down her softness. And his recently massaged muscles were ruined.

Then her little hands went exploring and feeling, and he jerked and gasped and groaned. And she panted and squeezed. She was hot and wet, and her tongue set his hair right on end. He knew it because he felt it. That wasn't all.

She about drove him over the brink! He wasn't too far gone to protect her, but it was a struggle to get her to leave him alone long enough to accomplish that. She was wild.

Then he was briefly stunned to realize that he was her first; and he tried to sort out what he ought to do about that, how to help her through the first onslaught; but she grabbed him and accomplished exactly what he'd wanted all along.

He sank into paradise. He breathed out a blast of scorching air and closed his eyes against the exquisite thrill of her. He held still to allow her time to adjust to the sensation. He struggled to raise himself off her, onto his elbows, and looked down into her widely opened eyes...and she grinned at him! She said, "Wow!"

"Oh, honey..."

"What do we do next?"

And he laughed. Helplessly, breathlessly. And he moved. "This."

"Oh, Angusss..."

She took to sex like a fish to water. She struggled and wiggled and squirmed and helped him right over the top and off into the most beautiful free-fall he'd ever taken, because she held him the entire way and it was together. It was just that: exquisite.

He'd once heard a man describe it that way: "exquisite." Now he understood. He didn't want to leave her. His body was wet with sweat. He was breathing raggedly. Laboriously, he lifted himself to his elbows again and put his forehead on hers as their bodies and breath recovered. She said "Mmm," as if she'd tasted something delicious. Did she think him delicious?

He asked her, "Are you okay?"

"Fantastic."

"You're that, all right."

"I mean it was fantastic."

"Yes."

She wanted to know, "When you kissed me last night, why didn't you do this then?"

His eyes crossed.

"Did you really want to now? Was I too bold? Are you okay? My word, it's amazing!"

"Yes." He had to agree to that.

"I'm not sure the manuals are quite clear on this."

"We'll do our own manual," he promised.

"We'd have to do a lot of research, keep notes, practice," she decided with a prissy sassiness.

He laughed. He really didn't want to leave her. "I don't want to leave you."

"Okay." She thought about it. "How do we fix lunch?"

"We give up eating."

"I believe I could exchange eating for something this marvelous, but eventually my stomach would start to growl. Would that be a turnoff?"

"Nothing would turn me off you."

"You're suggesting I get comfortable and adjust to this coupling for the rest of my natural life?"

He confirmed it. "Right."

"What a remarkable thing to do. I've been an idiot not to have tried it sooner."

"No!" A decisive response.

"Ah. You're getting territorial?"

"I've found evidence of such feelings ever since I found you sleeping in my bed, Goldilocks."

"I thought I was a goddess."

"That, too."

"How soon can we do it again?"

He lifted his head up and looked into her laughing eyes. "Now. It'll be a lot slower, and—this time—it'll be . . . exquisite."

"It was."

"Yes. You are. Can I be in love with you already?"

She didn't hesitate. "No."

"I'll be darned. When will love come?"

"We would have to be friends first, but I'm committed to finding . . . stolen children, you know."

"I hadn't known we had to be friends first."

She assured him, "It works best that way."

"Now, how can you know that?"

"My mother told me."

"What else did she tell you?"

"That when a man wakes up grouchy, a smart woman gives him breakfast in bed."

"So-o-o. That's what you were doing."

"I've never seen such a sore-eared bear."

"I'm sorry I was such a grouch."

"You're a very darling man."

"Darling? That sounds precious."

"You are."

"And you're a goddess," he said.

"We're back to that?"

"Yeah, Goldilocks, and I like having you sleeping in my bed."

"Me, too."

Very tenderly, he kissed her lips, which were softened and puffed by his attentions. "Is making love another remedy for grouchy men? This beats even breakfast in bed."

"No. Making love isn't a reward or a bribe. Mother was clear on that. It's a sharing."

"I like sharing with you in my bed."

She spread her heels wide and wrapped her arms around his waist, as she curled her body and opened her mouth under his.

He was willing to be coaxed back to passion. He was like a lazy lion whose lioness is ready; he pricks his ears in interest while she rolls and flirts.

Hillary loved the different textures of his body. The slickness of his drying sexual sweat. The roiling muscles under the smooth skin of his body, his hairy arms and legs, and the flare of hair on his chest. She moved her soft breasts and, trapped by his weight, they rolled against him.

As his interest mounted, he got up from her to lie beside her to explore her, taste her and look at her. A sensual feast. The scent of passion flared his nostrils, and his ears absorbed the sound of her sighs, the soft whisper of his hands on her, the slithering sounds of disturbed hair.

So leisurely were the preliminaries of the sated. There was no rush. There was time to relish their pleasure. Time to savor the nuances and pauses. Ah, the pauses as they gasped and their skins shivered with their delight. As they felt the thrills search out secret places and excite the sensitive tissue so exquisitely.

This was so different from the wild romp of their first time. And Angus knew it would be different from the next. Why was it so with Hillary?

He began a trailing tickle and watched her pupils dilate as her lips formed a surprised *Oh*. He smoothed his hand down her susceptible stomach and rubbed a hard, leisurely circle there. Then he reached farther, with a wicked finger swirl that made her gasp, as her whole body reacted in a sinuous writhing.

His tasting mouth explored, riveting her attention, and her head rolled in slow ecstasy as he learned her body, suckled at her breasts and explored her ears with a touching tongue. So lazy, so gentle, so titillating.

She learned of the coupling to tease, the separation to rest, and the time to enjoy. The pleasure sounds, the coaxing sounds, the sounds of intimate laughter.

But then her own curiosity urged her to touch and taste in turn. He was willing, and she was delighted with his response. But when he gripped the bed sheet with clawed fingers and flung back his head to suck air between his clenched teeth, she let go of him and sat back on her heels, alarmed. She quickly laid a compassionate hand on his chest and asked urgently, "Did I hurt you?"

He groaned and moved slowly, his eyes closed, his breath labored, as his lips formed the words "Do it again."

She laughed and scoffed, "You ham." Then she ruffled his hair, but he had other hair to ruffle and she did those places, too, across his chest and down his body.

They petted and patted; they smoothed and caressed. They kissed and played. And they made love, prolonging it, teasing, resting, loving beautifully.

But their passion mounted, and their interest slowly concentrated. Their hands became a little more demanding, their mouths greedier. Their breaths picked up in tempo. Hands were then a little harder, a bit stronger. The separations were quicker as they lay apart with panting breaths to calm somewhat. Then the recoupling was with building tension, teased and inflamed in the writhings of their slick bodies; fueled and fed with kneadings and tastings until they could not stop. They were feverish by then, their faces serious and intent. It was as if they struggled as they writhed in their hunger, and there was no other alternative but to rush on up that sensationally tumultuous spiral, with every cell concentrated, to reach the ultimate explosion in a wondrous starburst.

Angus thought *exquisite* was a nice word for some couplings, but there were other words. That one had been incredible. He was awed. Almost fearfully awed. He separated from Hillary and lay beside her carefully. She was a little pale; her eyes were closed, and her eyelashes looked black against her cheeks. Still trembling from his exertions, his breath still unsteady, he leaned on one elbow, hovering over her. "Are you all right?"

Her mouth curved into a slight smile; otherwise she didn't move. He kissed her cheek, almost in supplication, and he took up her limp hand and kissed it, too. He had to touch her. It was as if he needed reassurance that she was real.

Even as he gazed at her she went to sleep. He watched her for a while, and she slept exactly the way she had with his pill. He was a drug to her? He gave her such complete surcease that, with all she had riding on her shoulders, she could sleep that way? He smiled a little, then he kissed her so gently that she couldn't possibly notice...and her head slowly turned to him, as a sunflower to the sun. She'd done that twice before when she didn't even know him. And she had been a virgin, unused to being with a man, but she'd turned to him. It was with a strong emotion that he then—as gently—touched his lips to hers, and he felt the slight response as a strange stirring inside his chest.

He pulled the sheet over them and lay beside her, a possessive arm over her stomach, watching her even as he, too, fell asleep.

Willie called first. "Tate mentioned a clubhouse three times. Is there any significance to that?"

Hillary frowned in concentration and replied slowly, "Not that I remember."

"Think on it. With all the careful word usage, there are probably all sorts of clues. You'll have to listen to the tape again. I believe it's a deliberate dredging of your childhood memories. And Tate felt she had to be careful. She expected someone to search, maybe, so she's 'hidden' information that only you will know how to retrieve. You need to hear this and think. I'll bring it over now.'' She hung up before Hillary could demur.

The lovers scrambled to make themselves, and the bedroom, look as if they were only casual friends. Angus shaved. There was no way to disguise the beard burn on Hillary's face. She layered cover-up on her lightly tanned skin and looked as if she were wearing a complexion mask.

Dressed and waiting for Willie, Hillary tried to call Carter and all Tate's friends. But the phones either just rang or were connected to answering machines. Did those who had the machines listen to the tapes? What if they only listened every several days or so? There were no business phone numbers listed. So Angus and Hillary sent polite messages by special carrier to each of those residences to call Hillary Lambert at Angus's number. For replies, they would have to wait until Tate's friends got home from work. One of them must know something. At least who Carter was.

Willie came in with her witchlike, loose dark garments clinging to her slender body. Her eyes saw everything. Angus and Hillary might just as well have left the tumbled bed, beard and beard-burned face alone.

The three sat down and listened to Tate's tape to Boy. Angus went to sleep. Hillary almost did. Willie was riveted. Tate mentioned the clubhouse. She mentioned messages left in odd places. Some had been left in plain view.

When those comments came in the tape, Willie stopped it, marked it, replayed it and asked if Hillary remembered any of the messages specifically.

"I was the youngest. By the time Dad helped the others with the tree house, I was still too little to be of much use. I was a tagalong."

With hushed drama, Willie queried, "Tree house?"

"Yeah. Dad helped us to—"

"It wasn't just a clubhouse; it was a *tree house*?"

"That was a leftover from Tate's Tarzan period. Dad had made her a platform during that time, but the tree house was more elaborate. It was two-story."

Willie was fascinated, absorbing every word Hillary spoke.

"Where were the messages 'in plain sight'?"

"Oh, in the rooms. Where you see things all the time and never notice them. We played games that way in the house. My dad did that so we'd 'see' better. He'd hide a list of things in a room, give us a copy of the list and allow us the afternoon to find them all. It was great fun. He's a very clever man. Have you ever noticed the center of a poinsettia is like a bunch of matchsticks? One real matchstick isn't readily noticeable."

"What else?"

"What 'what else'?" Hillary asked.

"How were other things hidden?"

"Oh, a ring on the top of a table-lamp post, a cookie under a candlestick, an earring on a drape tieback. I can't remember them all."

"Tate has left you some message. We have to find it."

"Yes."

They listened again to the tape while they ate peanut-butter sandwiches for lunch. Angus slept on. Hillary racked her brain, adding memories but not solving anything. It was a long, restless afternoon. After a while Willie went home.

Hillary paced around. The urge to *do* something overwhelmed her. Having left Angus a note on the inside of his front door to say she was at Tate's, Hillary wandered around her sister's apartment, looking for something obvious. Something in plain sight. But if Tate had thought someone *else* would be looking, too, it would have to be cleverly in plain sight. Obvious only to Hillary.

Hillary groaned aloud, "Oh, Tate, I was never this clever. Surely you haven't staked everything on my understanding you. I never really did anyway. What have you done? How will I know?" And she was in despair.

Angus wakened and panicked when he found her gone. He was slumped on the couch. He immediately saw the sign on the door and surged up from the sofa to read that Hillary was at Tate's. He glanced around. Everything seemed in order. Rubbing away the crick in his neck—from sleeping in a crooked position—he went down the hall to find Hillary.

He tapped and waited. Apparently she did check the peephole, because she took her time opening the door. There were tears in her eyes. He asked quickly, "What's wrong?"

"I think Tate must believe I'm smarter than I am. I can't think of anything to help. Paul won't let us search for Carter, and I feel useless."

He wanted to say she was valuable to him but thought maybe she wouldn't appreciate hearing it right then. However, in her need for comfort, he had a legitimate excuse to hold her, and he did that with great pleasure.

She leaned against him, absorbing his sympathy—what she thought of as sympathy.

His deep voice rumbled in his chest as he told her, "Paul knows what he's doing. We need to go back to my place in case he calls there. We're going to know it all, and soon. Tate's friends still might help. They'll call. We need to be there in case one of them comes home early or has a different schedule. Come on, honey. Let's go back."

The phone in his apartment was ringing. It was Paul. "Carter's a woman. She hasn't been in her apartment for several days. She's missing."

Angus and Hillary looked at each other. Tate's backup. Gone. Where was Carter?

That made Hillary feel even worse. Tate had counted on her and Carter. "Without Carter, what am I to do? Where am I supposed to start?"

Angus said, "Wait."

And Hillary burst into tears.

Seven

With Hillary's tears, a remarkable metamorphosis began in Angus. He had been intrigued by Hillary from the minute he'd found her in his bed. Her missing sister was an additional interest. From his first glimpse of her, he'd wanted her with mounting desire. Now she began to capture his compassion.

It was with genuine concern that he took her hand and said, "We'll find them both."

"Carter was *supposed* to be here. He—she was the one I was supposed to contact, so she *had* to be available. She would have put a message on the answering machine if she'd had to leave unexpectedly. They're both being held. This must be something very important if they *are* both being held. Oh, Angus, what are we going to do? How are we going to save her?"

He called Finnig.

Hillary was shocked to her good-citizen toes. "You'd trust Finnig more than Paul?"

Really very mildly and with such good reasoning, Angus said easily, "Different contacts."

"I really don't approve," she informed him starchily.

"On rare occasions, there comes a time when it's any port in the storm. This is a storm. We need to know if Finnig can find out if anyone has seen anything—like one or two women being held somewhere. It would have to be in an out-of-the-way place, and it would have to be somewhere not connected with the people who are doing it; therefore, it is strange territory for the holders, too. They might have been seen...delivering food? Carrying bedding? Having electricity or water connected to a house that's vacant?"

Incredulous, Hillary demanded, "So *Finnig* is a safe harbor? Are we that desperate?"

He soothed her, "Let's not take chances."

"I think contacting Finnig is taking a chance."

"Trust me. I'm a good judge of how much to expect of any man."

She looked at him soberly and admitted, "I trust you with Tate's life."

"Oh, Hillary. Is it time to be in love yet?"

"You do know I'm committed to...my job."

"That's no problem."

In a surprisingly short time on that hot afternoon Finnig returned Angus's call. He had no trouble remembering who Angus was and was interested that the Carter whom Angus sought had disappeared. In his challenging mangling of the language, Finnig said something similar to "That sounds like my line. So describe her."

"How do we work the logistics?" Angus hedged.

"Exchange of information—nothing criminal or illegal. A favor. I might want to know if a ship's clean or riding the edge. That's all. Would you do it?"

So Finnig already knew exactly who Angus Behr was and what he did. Interesting. Angus demanded suspiciously in a hard tone, "Is this setting up a drug carrier?"

"No. It's legit. My word."

"You know the information is open to any caller?"

"I trust you," Finnig's wordage said.

"Okay. I'll vouch you five clearances on specific ships and crews. I'll guarantee them. That means I'll check them out myself. But if you work any damage on any of them, ship or crew, I'll get you."

"I was going to ask for two."

"This is important." Angus emphasized the words.

"I'll see to it myself."

"Deal. Her name is Tate Lambert. That's just to have as a label; she won't be wearing a sign. She's a thirty-five-year-old brunette, blue eyed, five feet eight inches, nicely built, stands straight, confident. She's a newspaper editor for the *People's Voice*. She does the women's page. We have no idea what happened or who took her."

"Know anything about Carter?"

"No."

"I'll get back to you."

Angus put down the phone and turned his head to look at Hillary. He said with some respect, "He's a businessman."

"I worry about this. Who are the good guys?"

"We're in heavy weather, and the seas are high. We need any help. Time is passing."

Hillary fretted. "This seems so unreal. It's so incredible. We're a middle-class family who are all really very ordinary."

"Yes. Of course. Everyone has a tree house. All girls are given men's names. That's what I knew in just forty-eight hours."

"It seems as if I came here two weeks ago. I can't believe this is all happening."

"Well, only for the sake of your believing, I shall do my best to make you realize this is all real." To do that his way, he kissed her.

But he really didn't have her attention. He felt that and lifted his head. "Don't worry. We're going to win through." He hugged her to him, holding her.

"I don't even believe you're real. I feel as if I'm in the middle of some fantastic dream and—"

"You find me fantastic?" He grinned at her.

"Angus, this is very serious."

"I know." He kissed her briefly. "Did you have lunch?"

"Peanut butter."

"Again? I haven't eaten. Come in the kitchen and watch me make my indescribable tuna delight."

She complained, "I feel as if I should be *doing* something."

"We have a great many people working on finding Tate. All sorts of people. The police. Finnig. Jim's contacts—and don't underestimate Willie."

"I feel useless."

Very tenderly he suggested, "Go take a nap."

"I couldn't possibly. Do you get to stay here, or will you have to go to work this afternoon?"

"I was listening to Tate's tape and I wonder—"

"You were asleep," she said.

"Not altogether. I was listening in a rather removed way. I heard Willie talk about hiding things in full view, and I wondered about Tate's computer. She might have left you a message on it. On a disk. I thought I'd go over her library and see if she's labeled anything for 'Boy' or 'Beanpole' or 'Tarzan.'"

"Oh, Angus. I should have thought of that."

"Fix me a peanut-butter sandwich? I'll go get the diskettes."

It took all afternoon. On the diskettes were a stunning number of short articles, a lot with names that could be germane. So each had to be brought up and scanned. Each was about a subject that was for the paper. It was like that—until they came to "Tree house," which was scrambled.

They looked through the rest of the diskettes, hurrying, taking the viewed ones back to Tate's apartment and carefully putting them away in sequence.

But they kept the one with "Tree house" on it, and Angus made four copies. It was the only one, on any of the catalogs they could find, that had been scrambled. They felt an excitement that stimulated them and made them feel they were helping Tate. Or at least, Angus felt he was doing something really solid for Hillary.

Hillary stared at the scrambled stream of uninterrupted, senseless letters and numbers and racked her brain for a code from the tree-house days. There *had* to be one. There had to be a key that unlocked the meaning of "Tree House." She questioned Angus, "Is Tate depending on me to remember a code? My mind's a complete blank. Would she expect that?"

"I doubt it. Why don't you go lie down for a while?
The others will be here this evening. We might be up
late tonight. Especially if we should get any other information."

"I'm antsy."

"I'll stay here, by the phone. Go down and swim
laps. You'll be safe. The pool's under a much more
alert security. No one's around. You'll just about have
it all to yourself. Swim until you're tired, then you can
sleep."

"I'll do it. But if anyone calls, you'll come out or
signal me from the window? Pull the drapes. I'll watch
for that."

"I promise," he said.

"Okay, then."

She'd brought her Speedo practice swimsuit because somehow Tate always had a pool available,
either in the apartment complex or nearby. A pool was
a must. There was nothing like a swim to relax tense
muscles, to drain away tension from the brain. Hillary changed, took up a towel and stopped to reach up
a kiss to Angus's mouth before she left.

That she would come to him so naturally to lift her
mouth for his kiss just about knocked him backward.
She did it so easily. And—obviously—she wasn't a
woman who had been intimately familiar with any
man before then. The simple, parting kiss was so
special that it meant almost as much to him as her
giving herself to him.

She smiled at him from the doorway, and he followed her. She went out and down the hall. He stood
in his doorway and watched her leave him, her straight
back, her beautiful feminine walk, a perfect woman.
As he looked down her long legs, he noted the cat was

blithely following her. He called to Hillary, and she turned back to wave, then she, too, saw the cat and laughed as she scooped it up and returned it to him.

"Why don't you let it follow you?" he asked with mock severity. "Maybe it would get lost and find another home." He took the cat from her arms, his hands deliberately grazing her breasts, making her *tsk* her tongue in scolding. He grinned and petted the cat, holding it in his arms.

"What a brutal man," she teased.

"Yeah." He smiled with his eyelashes screening the fires that leaped in his eyes. He could feel it happen. All through him. He had to be careful so she wouldn't think he was a sex maniac.

She kissed him again, sassily, then turned away and, since the hall was empty, walked in a swishing, flirting way, and she looked back at him to be sure he watched. His eyes were all the more avid because she was so unpracticed that she stumbled in executing her swish. He shook his head at her as he grinned, and she laughed.

Could it be love this soon? He was most certainly attracted to her as he'd never been to any other woman. He had to find her sister for her. He must. He would.

Hillary had taken her key, so he locked the door. He called Paul, Jim and Willie to say: "Found a scrambled message that might fit the problem." No names. He left the same message on the tapes for each of his friends.

Then he sat down at the computer and began to play with codes. He'd once seen a 1930s Little Orphan Annie code ring. A numbered wheel could be turned to set the number one on, say, the letter *e*, and then two would be f, three would be g, and so on. Simple. This one wasn't.

There was no call, the drapes weren't pulled in signal, so Hillary returned almost an hour later to unlock Angus's door and enter. He was still at the computer and so engrossed in the problem that he only subconsciously noticed her arrival.

She passed him on her way to the bedroom to change, and he continued to work at the puzzle. It wasn't until the phone rang that he surfaced to answer it. It was a woman who asked to speak to Tate's sister.

Angus went into the bedroom to find the cat sleeping crosswise on the center line with Goldilocks snugly asleep on his side of his bed. He shook her shoulder, saying, "Honey, there's a phone call for you."

She groped for the phone and said in a little-girl, sleepy voice, "Hello?"

It wasn't Tate. That's really what Hillary waited to hear: Tate's voice saying, "Hello, I'm free." Not Tate. The call was from one of her friends, who said, "Hillary? Well, hello! What are you doing in Chicago?"

And Hillary said, "I'm looking for Tate. Do you know where she is?"

"Is something wrong?"

Hillary replied carefully, "I can't seem to locate her. Have you heard from her lately?"

"No. It's been over a week or more, but that's not unusual. Will I get to meet you this time?"

And Hillary replied, "I hope so. Can you tell me Carter's first name? Or is that her first name?"

"It's Verna. She's such a— Is she missing, too?"

"Not that I know. I'm supposed to call her."

"She has an unlisted number. Tate will have it."

"Good. Thanks for calling."

"Keep in touch. If there's anything wrong, let me know. I would want to help."

"I'm sure everything's fine. But I'll have Tate call you."

"'Bye now."

Hillary hung up and saw that Angus had been listening. She said, "Carter's first name is Verna."

Almost immediately the phone rang again. There was the same questioning with the same results: good friends who offered to help if Hillary came up empty in her search for Tate's whereabouts. They all thought Hillary was in town as a surprise and just couldn't locate Tate right then. Hillary thought they all sounded like good women.

The calls were disappointing. Hillary hadn't realized how she'd counted on at least one of them being in Tate's confidence. It troubled Hillary that they weren't, for that implied that whatever had happened with Tate's disappearance, it might not be the piece of cake to solve that Tate's note had implied. Tate might have known it was chancy. Dangerous.

She told that to Angus, who said, "Don't borrow trouble."

But he was thoughtful, and his eyes were off as if he were considering something else and his attention wasn't entirely on what he was saying. Hillary shivered.

Angus found that nine was the filler between words, the substitute for the spaces. After that he searched for *e*, since it was the most commonly used letter in the English language. Eventually he figured out the really very simple code. The paragraph read: "Well, darling, I've gotten myself into a pretty mess. By this time you've contacted Carter, so you know what it's all about. Silly, isn't it."

Angus and Hillary lifted their gazes from the screen and stared at each other. What was silly? It was Carter who knew the vital next step. And Carter was missing.

It was then that they found that the code didn't work on the next paragraph or on any other. Maddening. There had to be some adjustment to the sequence that would allow them to continue. How clever. How irritating.

For supper they worked on the further depletion of Angus's stuffed freezer.

As they silently ate, Hillary paused in midbite and said, "I wonder if anyone else in the family remembers a tree-house code and how to adjust it."

"Brilliant."

"Why didn't I think of it sooner?"

"Because you're the youngest and you're used to taking orders, and Tate told you not to contact any of the others."

"I think you're probably right!"

She called the three other Lambert sisters and drew a complete blank. Georgina didn't appear surprised at all. Fredricka asked, "Tree house?" and Roberta asked, "Now what's Tate up to?" But Hillary couldn't answer; she couldn't even say Tate was missing. She said, "We're working on a code." That was certainly true. And she continued with complete honesty, "I just wondered if we'd ever had one, when we grew up."

Roberta laughed. "You two must be desperate for something to do! What's wrong with the male population of Chicago?"

After she'd talked to all three, Hillary hung up and sat with her hand on the phone, looking at Angus. "I wish they'd remembered the code. But how can I be angry with their faulty memories when I can't even remember if we had one at all?"

He comforted her: "We already know we're not going to find the information. Carter has it, and she's missing. We want to know the rest of what Tate left in the message for you, but it isn't going to help us to find Tate. Or to understand what this is about. Don't worry so, and quit blaming yourself."

Hillary mourned, "She depended on me."

"She depended on Carter. The rest of the message probably says: 'When you get the information, call the police.'"

"Tate would never do anything so fainthearted."

"Then she isn't the intelligent woman I've come to believe she must be."

Hillary confirmed, "She is."

"Then she'll tell you to call the police."

Critically, Hillary accused him, "I've never seen such a devotion to the police in any ordinary citizen."

"Your experience is limited."

"I've located a few children. The police have never been eager to assist me."

"Look at it from their point of view," Angus suggested. "You're looking for kids from a domestic involvement—that is, divorce. All cops loathe domestic squabbles. Good cops are uselessly killed in domestic fights. If they finally get a woman to file charges so they *can* get her man away from her and the kids, she drops the charges, he's freed, and it all begins again. They have more urgent things to do than to be referee in such unsolvable quarrels, And there's the human response of the uninvolved.

"In divorce, the child will be cared for by one or the other parent. There's seldom a clear-cut issue where one parent is right and the other's wrong. Both parents are entitled to know the child. Too often the quarrel over who has the child isn't entirely for the child's benefit; it's revenge on the partner that causes one parent to disappear with a child of divorce. It's a heartless tug-of-war. Neither parent 'wins'; only the child loses."

It was then that Hillary told Angus, "Tate has a child. A boy. His father took him away from her and has disappeared. It's been two years, and I'm committed to finding him. He's four years old now and starting nursery school. Tate's never even seen a picture of him in the whole two years. She has no idea where he is or what's happening to him. Or even if he's well or if he knows he has a mother who loves him."

Angus was frowning with his concern. "That's really tough. I'm sorry."

She nodded to acknowledge his words but went on: "That's how I got started. I look for Benjamin. Tate doesn't know if that's still his name. I'm going to find him for Tate."

Angus stood up slowly, came to Hillary and took her gently into his arms to hold her close. He murmured, "A bastard."

"They were married."

"I wasn't referring to the kid. Bastard has nothing to do with being illegitimate; it's a state of being. That is, the father doing such a rotten thing."

"I can agree to that."

"I'm sorry I spouted off like that. I feel bad for Tate. I know she never deserved such treatment from any man."

Unbelievingly, Hillary scoffed, "You don't even know Tate."

"I know an amazing amount about that unseen, unmet woman. That mounted fish says a whole chapter all by itself."

Hillary agreed, saying, "Benjamin is missing so much, not knowing Tate in these young, magic years."

"Honey, if Tate married this bastard, he *must* have socially redeeming factors. The kid will be okay."

"What about Tate?"

"How did she come to marry him?"

"He was mesmerized. He met her at a cocktail party. He's a hard-nosed businessman completely immersed in stocks, bonds, mortgages, liens, law, imports and exports, and investments. Whatever. She came into his orbit like a comet. He called her that.

"She's a strong woman. Almost too strong for most men. And she saw a man who was more powerful than she, who walked a wider, mysterious path, and she fell completely under his spell. She was willing to follow along, but for him she was simply an interesting pause along his way. He got her pregnant, married her as soon as they knew, and then he gradually was distracted from her by some fascinating deal that challenged him.

"He was furious when she divorced him. Then he took Benjamin. He had the decency to tell her it was he who had the boy. Tate was frantic. She grieves for Benjamin every day. She goes through hell."

"It must be exactly that, for Tate."

"If she only knew he didn't need her, or if she just had pictures. Dominic is forcing a cruel and unusual punishment."

"They all lose." Angus shook his head over the unsolvability of it all.

"Yes. Before I will search for a child, the parent must agree to share counseling, to sort things out, with another adult adviser in attendance who is on the child's side."

"That all costs money."

"The child's welfare is worth it."

"So you search for Benjamin?"

"Most of the time. Dominic is very wealthy. He leaves no trails."

"He hasn't left the planet. He's around here somewhere."

Hillary agreed. "And we Lamberts are persistent."

Holding her against him, he had become instantly conscious of her body close to his, but as their conversation went on, he was distracted from what was being said to only surface awareness. That consciousness of her body was narrowing his complete attention to the fact she was close enough that his body could feel her feminine softness. Her arms were loosely around his waist, her head on his shoulder; his knee had sneaked between her thighs. He lost the focus of her words...something about persistence.

He tilted his head down with his chin close to his chest so that his mouth could seek hers. She lifted her lips for his kiss, but it wasn't the soft salute she'd expected. His mouth tilted her head back as his raised to the dominant position, pushing her head against his arm while he turned that kiss into something spectacular!

She gasped at the surge of sensation that hit her and allowed his access to her mouth to deepen. He kissed her until all her senses were unreliable. Therefore, her knees were shot, her hands grasped with no real direction, and her eyes lost focus....

There was a knock on the door.

It took a while for them to realize that had actually happened and it wasn't the other's heartbeat gone completely out of control. They stared as their eyes gradually adjusted to reality. Then Angus stood Hillary on her boneless legs and patted her bottom with some pleased smugness. And incredibly, with her a complete shambles, *he went to open the door*.

Hillary stumbled into the bedroom as she heard Angus say with rather excessive heartiness, "Well, Paul, hello! Any news?"

Fortunately Paul's words were mumbled, because he wasn't holding his pad and pencil.

While Hillary was in the bathroom, pressing cold cloths to her face and trying to get back down to being reasonably normal, Jim and Willie arrived—having gone through security. When Hillary returned to the living room, they were crowded around the computer and each was making suggestions about the code. No one paid any attention to Hillary. So she could listen, amazed by their excitement for this additional challenge. Grateful for them.

A man is known by his friends. Somehow she knew these three weren't the limit of the people who cared about Angus. She sat and watched him, her head resting on the back of the couch under Tate's fish, the cat on her lap. Her idle fingers petted the cat where it wasn't licking as she watched the teamwork among the four gathered around the computer. Angus was the one who sat at it; his were the fingers that tapped in the variations of the code suggested.

They blundered onto the key to paragraph three, then figured out why. After that they could adjust the code for the other paragraphs and decipher the message. Tate had written:

Carter will have told you where to find everything I know. She doesn't know what it is, only where it can be found.

Take the info to Robert MacLean. Tell him to use his own good judgment in what should be done. I'm sorry I wasn't paying more attention. There's very little, as you see, but it'll give you a start.

My love to you, Boy. I'm sure there's no need for you to worry, but ten days is long enough.

The five people in Angus's apartment read it aloud a second time, then they were silent as they racked their brains.

Angus exploded in a rush of pent-up breath, "What in the hell could it be?"

Jim suggested, "A bloodless coup?"

"A takeover?" Angus tilted his head back and pushed up his lower lip.

Willie said, "How curious. She's not afraid, but she's not sure."

"Yes," Angus agreed.

"Who is Robert MacLean?" Jim inquired.

Hillary supplied the reply. "He's the real owner of *People's Voice*."

"Now, that lets in another facet. It would be news."

Angus laughed in appreciation. "All our busy minds, scrambling like mice for clues. Fascinating!"

Paul took out his pad and pencil and clutched them. "With taking Tate, they've broken the law."

"You want them caught," Willie declared with a shadow of an appreciative smile.

"Yeah." Paul was a little belligerent.

More softly, Willie added, "You don't want anyone to get away with anything."

Paul swung his head around and looked at her. "Nobody." And that included her, it was clear.

Jim said musingly, "We've done all we can. We're very nicely trapped into waiting. Any leads, Paul?"

"We're working on it."

"Anything coming to a boil in this next week or so?" Angus asked. "Tate guessed at ten days. In all the crises you mentioned of the political shenanigans, the murderer on death row, the corporation being investigated by the stockholders—what all. Any more on any of those?"

Paul replied, "Altogether there are five things coming to a head, in one way or the other, within these next two weeks. Big, nasty things that'll rock boats."

"Which one, oh, which one, oh, which shall it be?" Willie supplied with a shake of her head.

Paul said, "That's about it: guess."

Willie said thoughtfully, "And every one of them is something that will tamper with or correct a basic moral issue."

"That's the way it goes," Jim agreed.

Although it had been Jim who had replied, Willie watched Paul. She told him, "I'm going home."

And he replied, "I'll be along in a while."

As she left, Willie leaned and kissed Hillary's cheek, then smiled into her eyes and said, "I'm glad."

Hillary shot a look at Angus, who simply looked smugly pleased. He'd *told* Willie? How shocking.

So Jim, too, kissed Hillary's cheek. It was like an initiation. An acceptance? She was torn between being indignant that Angus would tell them something so intimate and touched that they had accepted her as one of them. What strange people.

Paul didn't leave. The other two went on out, with Jim grousing about having to check out with security as they disappeared down the hall.

Angus closed the door and turned to Paul. "So?"

"We're running into other inquirers, those who are working for Finnig. Why waste my people's time?"

"He's that thorough?"

"Very." Paul nodded once.

"Then let him do it."

Sourly, Paul asked bluntly, "What are you giving for this . . . giving from Finnig?"

"Five guaranteed clean ships. You know he came here. I told you that. He expected to find only Hillary. I surprised him. But he knew my moles and birthmarks by the next day!"

"Clean . . . ships?"

"This will surprise you even more. He gave his word."

"Finnig going legit?" Paul stepped an elaborate step backward to mime astonishment as he put the hand holding the pad and pencil to his heart.

It was the first time Hillary had seen Paul act anywhere near his age. He was probably thirty-three, but he generally acted as if he were twenty years older. She smiled at his attempt at humor, but her mind was intrigued by the fact that Paul was going to Willie's. Willie didn't like a foul mouth. Did Paul make love to her clutching that pad and pencil? Or did he just keep his mouth so busy he didn't have to talk?

Paul told Angus, "Put the 'Tree House' diskette back. It doesn't give them any information, and we have a copy. Put it back."

"Carter. It tells about Carter."

"They've got Carter," Paul said.

"How do you know?" demanded Hillary.

"She was seen with Tate the last anyone saw of Tate. She's missing. So is Tate. We assume when Tate was taken, Carter was there and they included her. At the very least, she saw the snatching and they didn't dare not take her. That's what we think."

"Incredible." Hillary gasped. "Who?"

And Paul said quietly, "We'll find out."

Paul finally left. He, too, had kissed Hillary's cheek. It was like being knighted, she thought. Did they knight women yet? Paul had knighted her. They had made her one of them.

Eight

After Paul left, the lovers eyed each other. There was a little smile on Angus's smug face. He was feeling cock-of-the-walk. It had pleased him enormously that the diverse, critical three had accepted Hillary so readily, so soon. They'd never managed any such acceptance of Pat.

Hillary said with prim stiffness, "I'm shocked you would tell them."

"About 'Tree House'?" His voice was tender. "They needed to know what Tate said. Weren't they brilliant?"

"Yes. But for you to tell them about us!"

That surprised him. "I never said a word."

"Then how did they know?"

He tried to smother a chuckle. "You have to remember Willie came over this morning. She saw your beard-burned face. And she had to notice I was walking different. Strutting a little, maybe. I was so pleased that you'd love me. I guess I couldn't hide that."

"You didn't tell any of them? Why did they kiss me?"

"You're one of us."

She nodded. "That's exactly how it seemed," she admitted. "That they had accepted me. But I thought maybe they were just being kind because I'm so scared about Tate."

"I think that Tate could come through this okay."

They had moved into the bedroom and begun to prepare for the night. It was so natural to chat along as if doing that *was* natural. Hillary said, "Weren't you surprised that Paul backed off and is letting Finnig do the searching? It makes me a little indignant that Paul would quit."

"No. Paul's allowing Finnig to take over just that hunting aspect. That frees Paul's people for something else. When you work, you use the tools at hand. Finnig is a handy tool right now. He has the network to search. Paul understands that. Finnig's people can be less obtrusive in their looking than the cops."

"It's strange to have Finnig on our side."

"He's positive that whatever Tate is involved with has nothing whatever to do with any of his... activities."

Hillary could understand that. She speculated, "Tate must have stumbled onto one of those three things Paul mentioned. Probably one of two. The corporation mess or the political mess. Which do you think?"

Angus replied positively, "In mysteries it's always the least obvious one." He walked over to the bedroom window to look out over the night-lights that shone along the curving shoreline. He went on: "The incident that has ensnared Tate is logically the political mess. Newsworthy. Shocking. Someone got something on someone in that bunch that's going to alter the balance of power. The politician isn't actually involved. But it's going to stink to high heaven.

"If they can hold back the revelation until he can perfectly word himself into a distance from the happenings, he might survive. It's going to be one of the underlings that's revealed as having been caught selling clout or doing some manipulating. That's where I'd put my money down."

He turned his head to look at her, and he wore a cynical grin. "But it could be the corporation in question. Both men are powers, but there is one stockholder with votes in his pockets who hates the guts of the board chairman, and he'll probably bring the company down around their ears with this fight. An image-harming private quarrel made public. Too bad."

"I wonder how Tate found whatever she found."

"We'll know within the next few days." He took off his shirt. "Want the bathroom first?"

"I suppose *now* I could use your toothbrush?" She gave him a knowing look.

He laughed. "You only now know why I asked?"

"You cad! How could I be diseased? What about you?"

"I'm pure."

She laughed a delicious chuckle. "My mother quoted a marvelous New York stage actress who claimed to be 'pure as the driven slush.' Does that shoe fit you?"

He smiled tenderly. "I really believe it's love already."

"Nonsense. It's the excited tension of adventure. As soon as this is over, you'll look at me and you won't see a goddess—you'll see an ordinary woman."

"Really?"

"Oh, yes," she assured him.

"Then what?"

"You'll suggest the danger is through and it's time for me to move back to Tate's apartment. Just so I can visit with her for a while before I return to Kansas City."

"I'd do that?" he asked.

"Of course. You'll do it with smooth regret, saying for me to take my time moving out, that you'll be gone for a few days checking barnacles or something on ships going down the St. Lawrence."

He held up a hand. "Wait. I have to write this down. I can probably sell it to a guy I know and Xerox it off and make us a tidy fortune. Tell me the exact words."

"You idiot."

He pretended to write. "Y-o-u i-d-i-o— One *t* or two? Isn't that an insulting way to start off?" He looked up with great, earnest interest. "I'd think a man in this situation would be a little more tactful. How about saying, 'Honey, it's been fun'? I know of a guy who actually *said* that. We can think of a better address. Put your mind to it. Anybody who could figure out looking for barnacles on a ship down the St. Lawrence has to have an inventive mind." His watching eyes were level on her. His face was serious. "Don't go inventing exit lines."

The look lasted awhile. She wondered, what did he see in her? He was such a superior man. He was so...in control. He was so brilliant and worked so hard. How could she have been lucky enough to have blundered into his apartment? How many times does a nine fall over and an apartment-six key fit the lock of a nine's door? And he could have been any kind of man, but he was Angus Behr. How astonishing. However... She was committed to the search for Benjamin, and she would continue to search just as diligently as she always had. Of course, there were the in-between times. She smiled and said, "I wish I had a pretty nightgown."

He swallowed a little audibly and licked his lips before he could suggest, "You could go without."

"You jest! The fact that I've slept with you is incredible. To actually go *naked* is too much. Much too much. You get me in T-shirt and white cotton pan—"

"I'll take you."

She laughed delightfully and went to brush her teeth—with her own toothbrush.

When she came from the bathroom, the top sheet had been thrown back and he was stretched out on the bed. The cat was on the other side of the bed—her side—also stretched out, licking, licking, licking. Angus informed Hillary seriously, "You can't move her. She was here first, and that's her half of the bed. She's shared for three nights now, and that's asking a whole lot of a cat who can only listen and lick. You'll have to share my side of the bed."

"I believe you warned me about crossing the center line. You implied I'd be wrecked."

"People can't live staid lives. It's worth a risk now and again to taunt the chances."

She expressed rather elaborate surprise. "I didn't know that."

"You have a lot to learn. We might just as well get started." He contrived to sigh in a put-upon manner.

As any traveler does, she surveyed her alternate routes. Blocking her way, he was lying along the edge of the bed, clothed only in pajama bottoms. He was looking up at her, one foot bracing an elevated knee in place. Green eyes watched her with lazy delight, his lips quirked with his humor. His chest was bare with a light covering of hair swirls that made her fingers twitch to play there.

To share his side of the bed, she would have to climb over him. He made that clear. She could take the coward's way and go around the bed to board there, but he'd said risks were sometimes needed.

She decided on the direct, risky route and approached the bed.

He lifted his far leg up and propped it on the raised knee, effectively barricading the bottom of the bed. She would have to take the northern route, which crossed his stomach.

She put her hands on her hips, narrowed her eyes at him and pulled her amused mouth into a disgusted look. "You're a sneaky man."

"Why are you surprised? You could have asked me if I was sneaky." He was amazed she would be so dense. "I'd have told you that anytime you wanted to know. I'm open and aboveboard." He smiled at her unfairly. "Which way are you going to take?"

She hesitated, knowing what would happen as soon as she moved toward him. "Put your legs down straight."

He did that fairly well, laughing.

And she had to laugh with him. He was wicked. So she then said, "Put your hands behind your head. Don't move."

He slowly obeyed. His quick tongue licked his lips; his green eyes danced with emerald flames as he watched her every move with such intensity.

She prolonged it. Moving slowly, she lifted her knee to slide across him, but he simply raised his leg, and she found herself trapped astraddle that strong barrier. She said, "Uh-oh."

His arms enclosed her, pulling her down on top of him, his mouth taking hers. Holding her, he rolled so that her floor-anchored foot was lifted free and she was helpless.

She lifted her mouth away from his and looked into green fires. She whispered, "Help, help."

He laughed a wicked, wicked rumble, and, holding her tightly to him, he rolled her over and onto her back—directly over that dangerous center line—and under him. He kissed her until her head began to swim, her eyes were unseeing and her mouth wore a silly smile.

Having kissed her giddy, he pushed up from her clutching arms to sit back on his heels. With his knees on either side of her thighs, and her legs trapped beneath him, he took off the T-shirt that covered her so unnecessarily. Then he moved back, crouching, and slid those utilitarianly protective white cotton panties off her hips and down her legs to join her T-shirt on the floor.

She watched his pleasure in looking at her, lying there stark naked, in nothing but a spectacular blush.

He smiled into her blue eyes and turned his head in one short half shake as he said, "Fantastic."

She put out her hands to cover her face, and his rumble of amusement made her smile in turn, but the spectacular blush turned gloriously scarlet. She felt his movement and peeked to see what he was doing.

The cat had become annoyed by the jiggling bed and left as Angus stood up on the bed and pulled the cord tie to release his pajamas. He let them drop, then kicked them aside. It was he who was spectacular. Beautiful. Her busy, staring eyes darted and paused and rounded. In her budding sexual vocabulary, she had only one word, already used, and she said it again. "Wow."

He was willing to accept "wow" very kindly. He came down on hands and knees to stretch up to her mouth to kiss her. Then, kneeling there, he watched his exploring tanned hands move along her white flesh, and his heated body began to film with sexual sweat. For a relatively average woman, she appeared to have a lot of points of interest, for it seemed to take him an unusual amount of time, and she became restless and wiggly so that he said, "Hold still."

Finally, as he moved, the opportunity came, and she boldly reached to cup him in an exceedingly intimate way. She really caught his riveted attention fast. The air whooshed from his lungs, to be dragged back in a quick, deep gasp, and he became remarkably tense and trembly. His reaction fascinated her, so she did it again even more intimately. Then she used both hands.

At her touch he'd released her and swiftly straightened. He immediately left the bed to go into the bathroom and came back with the packet. She thought it was her turn to explore, but he had suddenly became very single-minded and intently hurried. He stayed out of reach until he was prepared. Then he pushed her back, and his body covered her as he thrust hotly into her burning depths. He paused, shivering for control, but it was too late, and he took them both on a quickened ride to glory—which burst into a million beautiful fragments, leaving them limp and gasping and deliciously spent.

When her breath came back under control and she could speak, she groused, "I wasn't ready."

He laughed in helpless gasps.

"You had all the fun." Her words were slow and carefully formed with tired lips. "Looking and touching. I didn't get to do anything."

He rubbed his whiskery face tiredly into her throat. "I had to show you how. You get a free hand next time."

"I'm a quick learner. I could have had a hand in this one." Her words were mumbled.

He separated from her with slow movements and fell to the bed beside her. He complained, "I've created a maniac. I'll become a love slave to a voracious woman; helpless, used."

"Not right now."

"Here's your main chance. I'm defenseless before your carnal will."

"I want to choose my own time."

"Will you warn me? Or will you just attack?"

"I'll have to see," she said.

"Kiss me good-night."

She smiled. "You starting something?"

"I knew it! Just kiss my cheek."

"How about . . . if I should kiss you . . . there."

"Nothing," he scoffed. "I'm sated."

"How about . . . there?"

"Why, Hillary Lambert!"

"Or...there?"

"How about here?"

"May I?" She smiled.

"Be my guest."

"Do you mind?"

"I'll have to see. Try it."

She shifted and delicately kissed him, then she looked up at him and smiled. Her eyes were shadowed by her heavy lids and screening lashes. Her hair was a wanton tangle. Her cheeks were reddened by his attentions, as were her soft breasts. Her pink-and-white naked body was languid and curled so femininely around his contrastingly hard, hairy, masculine form. She was a siren.

He laughed again softly in silence, his eyes kindling. "It isn't possible."

But apparently it was.

In the morning the pair smiled and loved each other in yet a different way. Hillary had early calls from friends of Tate's asking if there was any news. And Angus had calls from the three other investigators.

It was after breakfast that Hillary went over to Tate's apartment for some creme rinse and found that the place had been entered and Tate's diskette files removed. All of them. Angus called Paul, who said, "Good. They probably have Carter. They'll have no idea we know about 'Tree House.' They'll feel secure."

"Any clue who they are or where Tate is being held?"

"Not yet."

After that conversation was finished, Angus said to Hillary, "Have you ever noticed the words he uses? He didn't say there were no leads; he said, 'Not yet.' I like a positive man.''

''Would they make Tate decode 'Tree House'?''

''I don't know.''

To reassure themselves, they put the copy of ''Tree House'' back on Angus's computer in order to read it again. Angus told Hillary, ''If they have Carter, as it appears they do, then they should feel confident they still have full control. With Carter in their clutches, any investigation is stymied at the first step. They'll feel safe.''

Again they spent the day at the apartment. Angus went to his office briefly to drop off letters for his secretary, to be briefed on current investigations and to gather things on which he could work at home. Then he went to the library and checked out tapes of newspapers, of the *People's Voice*, to see if there was any unusual story they could find that might be a hint of what Tate had found. And on his way home, he stopped at the grocery to replenish their supply of frozen dinners.

While Angus got a great deal done that day, Hillary hit a low point of activity. Viewing the files, she noted date and page of several things straight out of left field, but they were so remote that she didn't feel anything was germane.

The two took turns swimming so that one of them was by the phone. And the cat seemed glad to have the people around. It was more interesting. Angus was marvelously contented, while Hillary was restless and frustrated. She felt useless.

After an enhanced frozen shrimp-creole dinner and the last of Mary Jane's perfect bread, they had watermelon for dessert. And it wasn't long before Paul arrived. Then came Jim and finally Willie in her witch's clothes, looking mysterious.

They all again kissed Hillary's cheek but in a rather absentminded way. Willie said, "I saw a friend of mine. She says Tate is well. She's in a murky place with machinery that's rusted. She's with men who are disguised."

Paul took out his pad and pencil and held them to take notes. It was his most serious stance. "Disguised?"

"I believe her exact word was 'distorted.'"

Hillary had heard of police consulting psychics, but she was incredulous that Paul would appear to take Willie seriously. Then she looked at Willie. She, too, took it very seriously.

Willie said, "I feel there is a game being played. One that isn't involved. I see Tate at a table. She's wearing something soft. It's cool."

Paul said, "Machinery, huh?"

"Rusty machinery."

"We'll take a peek around."

Angus said, "Won't you tell Finnig?"

"Of course. We've set up a communications system that puts us in touch."

Angus laughed and Jim grinned. Paul could not abide tainted people.

Jim apologized for turning up more gossip: some concerned a bank employee, a racket fleecing the elderly that had been widespread and exceedingly lucrative, and the one witness had vanished.

That caused them all to straighten—it would be just like Tate to wade into something like that—but, Paul said, the witness had been seen after Tate had disappeared. It wasn't Tate.

There were other things, things that were important to the people involved but not of a wider interest. The four told Hillary that they felt such internal squabbles or dishonesties wouldn't warrant the taking of a hostage.

However, there were the other crises still not in public knowledge. No doubt such existed all over the country, but of the two in Chicago, Paul reported that it looked as if the politician could be dragged down with the scandal. The first rumors were beginning to circle, and noses were being lifted to the odor of dirty dealings. There was nothing so disastrous to public welfare as a trusting, charismatic candidate who charmed and gathered followers but was too naive to be a good judge of character in his supporters.

There were very greedy, questionable men riding on the political coattails, and they would do almost anything to see to it the candidate survived—for their own purposes. If Tate had found something to do with this mess, she could be in serious trouble.

It was Jim who knew the most about the corporation hurrying toward disaster. Only because he happened to know socially the two men involved at the center of the struggle: two power-struggling, ruthless apples in a barrel of honest people. There, too, it could be very tricky for Tate. They might hesitate to harm her, but it wouldn't be beyond them to arrange something. Especially the vote-holding stockholder, who was an unbendable man.

But...

Ah, the four agreed, that was the problem. There were alternatives. The snatchers might well be connected with something totally unrelated. It could be something not yet known. And that was the most

dangerous threat of all to Tate. The unknown. Then
if anything happened to her, unknown was untrace-
able.

Hillary said that night to the others, "I think my
biggest problem is not being able to *do* something to
help."

Jim replied, "You have to know we're all almost in
that same boat. We've found probable causes. But we
don't know how to search and find a stolen woman.
This would be almost impossible for you alone, because it's so different from your stolen-child searches.
There are no names to trace, no utilities connection or
phone numbers to find. No jobs through which people can be located. Not even the general area of inter-
ests of the people we're trying to find. Finnig is
looking. If Tate's anywhere in the city, he will know
shortly. They have to eat. They need things. We'll find
out. If she's on a boat—"

"I have men looking." That was Angus's calm
voice.

"Good for you," Willie said. "There must be a
million boats around the lake. Boathouses."

"All are being checked." Angus looked at Hillary
to reassure her. "It takes time."

Paul nodded. "Good. Good." Then he, too, looked
at Hillary. "Patience."

She sighed. "It's very hard."

"I have a lot of mug books for you to idle through.
All the people who've had their pictures taken by the
police. You might do a study on people who get in
trouble."

"I want to do something for Tate."

"You called me." Paul saluted that.

"I told Angus not to," she admitted.

"I know."

"I'm sorry."

"Since Angus didn't pay any attention to that, we got on the case almost as soon as if you'd called from Kansas City." With such courteous words, he was holding pad and pencil.

"All we do is listen for the phone," Hillary lamented.

"Police work takes a lot of interviewing, searching and patience. But someone has seen something in this city that could lead us to Tate and solve it all fast."

"Safely," Hillary said.

Paul nodded. "That's the way we work."

And another day went by. Lying on his side of the bed, locked in his arms, she was pensive. "I'm not sure I'm being loyal to Tate in enjoying sex with you while I don't know where she is."

"How would abstaining help?"

"Are you a justifier?" she asked.

"I have to pay attention to my own welfare," he said, explaining his stand logically.

"Like the politician's followers?"

"I'm not devious."

She disagreed, "Oh, yes, you are. You teased me with the center line."

"That was open and aboveboard. I did warn you."

She complained, "Then you taunted me about taking chances."

"That was only to expand your life and times."

"You snared me in with your clever talk."

He smiled. "I think we've cured the cat from sleeping on the bed with us. She gave up last night and hasn't been back. We might think about sleeping on the table next, and that way—''

The phone rang. It was Finnig. In his inimitable version of English, he said approximately, "I just wanted you to know I'm working on it."

"Anything interesting?"

"It's a busy city. Ask Paul if there's a sting operation south of me."

"I'll get back." Angus hung up and punched in Paul's number. After it rang awhile, he called Willie's. "Paul there?"

And Paul asked colorfully what Angus required.

"Not holding pencil and pad?" Angus asked sweetly, and held the phone away from his ear until the sputtery sounds died down. "Finnig wants to know if you have a sting operation south of him."

"It's an illegit fence."

"Oh, ho! I'll tell him."

"Tell...Finnig to keep his...nose clean until this is finished."

Angus called Finnig and told him both responses.

Finnig growled, "He knows I'm legit," and hung up.

Angus lay down again beside Hillary and took her back against his hot body. "Too bad those two aren't on the same side. They'd be great complementary friends."

"One of my sisters is a lawyer. When she was in law school, the class was taken to a penitentiary. There were some sections in the prison where they allowed no women at all. Only the male students went there. They said the caged men were animals. But in one of the prisoner gathering-places, through the bars, one of the law students saw a childhood friend from his old neighborhood.

"They stared at each other, and neither greeted the other. It really shook the student. Back at school, he kept exclaiming over his childhood friend being in *that* place. 'We grew up together. We had the same childhood. We did the same things. There wasn't any difference between our families. There but for the grace of God was I. I could have been there!' Roberta said he was days getting past that. Of the two of them, how had he been the lucky one?"

Angus's fingers were idly playing in the silk of Hillary's hair. "Everything influences us. I wonder how seeing his friend in that terrible place will influence the lawyer in his own life. With his own children. Probably the biggest thing anyone can learn is that it's never too late to stop doing what's wrong and change their lives into the way they want them to go."

"Do you think Finnig is doing that at his stage of life?"

"He wants legitimate boats and crews. We'll all be watching him like hawks."

"And he's helping to find Tate."

Angus commented, "I wonder why."

"You think he has an . . . angle?"

"Men like Finnig don't do things for charitable reasons. But in these circumstances, I wonder why he'd put all his people out to search for a woman who has no real clout."

"Maybe it's for the good of his soul?"

"I'd doubt he has one."

"Then why?"

"I can't figure it. None of us has any real pull. I doubt he's trying for Brownie points with the police.

I've only done my normal job in guaranteeing him clean ships. Who is he trying to impress?''

"Maybe he just wants to help us."

"Finnig?" Angus's tone supplied the word with a wealth of incredibility.

And Hillary said, "Yes."

"Don't bet the rent money."

Nine

The next morning it seemed to Hillary that there was a tension in the air. Her nerves seemed to vibrate. She opened her eyes and looked around. If there'd been a darkly shrouded stranger standing in the room, she wouldn't have been surprised. She sat up and listened.

"What's the matter?" Angus watched her.

"I don't know. It's as if I know something is going to happen. But I don't know what."

After a minute Angus said, "I have a suggestion."

She brought her glance over to him and stared. Slowly her attention came back to their situation and she smiled. "What you'd suggest under these circumstances is about what I'd expect from you. How did I land in a sex advocate's bed?"

He curled closer. "How do you know I wasn't going to suggest swimming?"

"It never occurred to me, somehow."

"See? Who's the sex advocate?"

Thoughtfully she admitted, "I believe you've converted me."

"Have I." He smiled marvelously.

She ran her fingers along his bare and hairy chest. "I like touching you. You're so different."

"From what?"

"Me."

He pretended astonishment as his glances quickly and elaborately compared their bare bodies. "Why, I'll be darned! We *are* different. I'd never noticed. I suppose I was so stunned after you'd first jumped me, and so exhausted since then, that I just didn't have the chance to pay attention." He rubbed his palm over her sensitive breasts and frowned. "You're very oddly lumpy. What causes these lumps? That must have been a hell of a mosquito to leave a welt like that. How nice that they're balanced. One could have been here and the other on your forehead."

She listened with great interest and then explained, "I don't know what causes them. I haven't always had them. They just started growing. And they're a dreadful nuisance. They bounce and swing and jiggle. They push out over the table. I run into people with them. And men especially gasp in indignation."

"They jiggle? Show me what you mean."

So she jiggled, and that *fascinated* him. He held them so they were still. She thanked him for helping out. He said "Anytime."

Then she said, "Since you feel free to question, I've been longing to ask, but of course, I really didn't want to make you feel self-conscious. However, I am so curious: what in the world did that to you?"

He looked down to see what interested her to that degree and raised his glance to her eyes to reply blandly, "When I was just a little tyke—I think, oh, about five or so—I saw I was different from my little niece, who was a year younger than I, and I asked my daddy just that question. My daddy said my mother had been scared by a snake."

She had to bite her lip before she could speak without too much of a wobble. "Oh. That makes sense. Prenatal influence." But then she had to cough a little.

"Well, I wasn't exactly sure, because I'd caught my daddy in some big hoaxes. Like he'd be mad at me and he'd say he was going to jump down my throat, and I could see he was too big for that. So I went to my mother. My daddy followed me and stood in the doorway. Mother leaned over with her hands on her knees, and she listened to me, as she always does. Then she wanted to know, 'Why do you ask that?' And I told her Daddy said the reason I was different from my niece was because my mother had been scared by a snake."

Her blue eyes brimming with delight, Hillary asked, "What did your mother say to that?"

"She looked up at my daddy for a while, smiling, then she began to laugh, and he did, too. She went over to him and reached up and ruffled his hair, and he hugged her. They just seemed to forget all about my question, so I squirmed in between them and demanded to know if it was true that she'd been scared by a snake, and she said, 'Yes!' She and Daddy laughed together. I felt left out."

Hillary sympathized, "Aw," and pushed her fingers through his hair. Then she said, "I'm glad your mother had that fright. I think the mark it left is beautiful.''

"Do you? I suppose. But it's a terrible nuisance. It gets restless sometimes. But I've heard it *can* be helped," he confided with an earnest look.

"Really?"

"Yes," he confirmed solemnly. "There are treatments. I've heard it can be helped by a good, compassionate, dedicated woman. I was hoping...that perhaps *you*'d have a kind heart."

"For the good of the community?"

He nodded.

"Well, I suppose everyone should do his share."

"Hers," he corrected quickly.

"That does narrow it down."

"You'll help me?"

"As a good citizen, however recently I've become a citizen of Chicago."

"That's big of you."

"I'm not the one with the problem," she reminded him.

He volunteered in turn, "I could work on your mosquito bites."

"An *exchange*!"

He smiled.

But at 8:27, when Hillary wakened again, sexually sated, it was with the same feeling of tension that something was going to happen.

Angus felt her restlessness and tightened his arms and kept his eyes sealed shut, hoping she'd go back to sleep. She peeled herself from his persistent embrace and picked her T-shirt up off the floor to pull it over her head. She and the cat prowled around the apartment, looking out the windows, glancing impatiently at the phone.

Angus came from the bedroom, pulling on his pajama bottoms. He tied the cord and stood there half asleep, doing his best to stand upright and try to keep her company. She was charmed. She went to him and hugged him. He pretended to snore, leaning some of his weight on her slender body, his forehead bent down to the top of her head. She laughed at him.

He stepped back with sleepy care and stretched, yawning hugely. His precarious pajama trousers slid down his hairy stomach to catch on the snake mark. And Hillary smiled a little as she admired the beautiful male body he was displaying for her in such a cocky way.

He brought his arms down slowly, moving his shoulders back and forth as if they were stiff, and he saw her watching him.

She laughed, and he reached out and pulled her to him to hug her. "Ah, Hillary, is it now that love comes?"

"Not yet."

So they were still at breakfast at 10:27 when the phone rang. It was Finnig. Angus interpreted his sounds to mean: "Something's come up. Be ready. A couple of men'll come to the door downstairs. They'll say 'Finnig,' and one's Mark and the other Phillip. Got that? They won't come inside."

"When?"

"After ten tonight. Be there. Angus, don't tell nobody."

"Right."

Angus put the phone down and looked at Hillary. "We're to be ready tonight at ten, outside the building. Two men—one will be Mark and the other Phillip. They'll say, 'Finnig'—that's how we'll know them. We're to go with them."

"To Tate?"

"Apparently."

"He didn't say specifically?"

"No." Angus shook his head. "Only that we are to go along with Mark and Phillip."

"Where?"

"He didn't say."

"Tate must be all right." Hillary's eyes were enormous. "If she wasn't, there would be no reason for us to go along. I'll see Tate tonight!"

"We'll see," he hedged.

"Are you going to phone Paul?"

"Naturally." He turned to dial.

"No!"

Angus looked over at her. "I must. Paul has to know where we are at all times."

Hillary argued, "If we're followed, Finnig might pull out. Did he tell you to phone Paul?"

He evaded. "I must call him."

"Finnig told you not to, didn't he? Specifically, he said not to."

"Yes." He raised his head and looked Hillary straight in the eye. "But I am going to call him. Paul has great sensitivity to balance. He has good judgment. He'll know how to handle this. If he thinks it would harm our chances, he won't have us followed, but if he smells a rat, he will. I trust Paul. And if we vanish, he'll know who to tap."

"Send him a note."

"The way Tate did." Angus's stare was deliberate.

"Yes."

"And where would you be now if Paul hadn't been contacted?"

Hillary declared, "Paul has been no help at all. He's spent a lot of time eliminating possibilities, while— alone—I would have followed leads that were apparent. He interviewed Robert MacLean, but Mr. MacLean knew even less than we do about Tate's research. Paul's interview only allowed Tate's boss to know she was missing. I would have done that when Carter didn't turn up.

"Tate knew what she was doing, *and all along she said not to call the police.* It is Finnig who has helped, and it was he who contacted us after we went to the hospital to search for Carter. After twenty-four hours, I would have searched for Carter in hospitals and morgues on my own."

Rather stiffly, Angus capsulized: "Then you don't need me. You would have been with Tate sooner, too. You forget that Paul made me stay here and take care of you. Whoever has Tate had free access to that apartment. When they came for the diskettes, they'd have taken you, too."

"Not necessarily," she countered. "They could have taken the diskettes without going into the bedroom. They probably wouldn't even have known I was there."

He almost snarled, "With 'I'm on my way' on the phone tape?"

"Well . . . I'm not sure they would have listened to the phone tape."

"Whoever took Tate is not of the ordinary criminal mode. Paul and Finnig both agree on that. Neither one has any rumble or rumor about anyone like Tate being snatched. It's an amateur job. These kind of people all have home answering machines *and they listen to them automatically.* So you have Paul to thank that you're not with Tate."

"That I'm here in your bed."

"That has nothing to do with anything but us. That was the greatest of miracles. I wouldn't have met you if maintenance had been a little sharper. But without that miracle, you would have gone along on your own, *and you too would be a hostage* in whatever madness it is in which Tate is involved. Don't kid yourself for a minute that you wouldn't. And since we're dealing with amateurs, I'm going to keep the pro informed."

"I forbid it."

He looked at her. Her mouth still bore the residual puffiness of his lovemaking. Her eyes were intent. She had taken in a deep, violent breath and was holding it. She was adamantly committed to preventing his call to Paul.

She was precious to him. This stranger, this Goldilocks, whom he'd found in his bed. He couldn't defy her. If he had to go out into the wilds of Chicago with Finnig's "boys" to places unknown, without a friend to back him, he would do that for her. It was exactly as he'd thought. She was in trouble, and he was putting his fragile human body on the line for her. Every time.

Time. He had until ten that night. He did have some time. He put down the phone.

She immediately burst into tears. She cried raggedly and flung herself into his arms... and he held her. This idiot woman who didn't know one thing about the seamy side of life. A woman on whom God smiled continuously, who was determined to walk into a dark pit fraught with unknown dangers. Going with

two cohorts of Finnig's—which was no recommen-
dation *at all*—and Angus Behr. Idiocy. Pure, unadul-
terated idiocy. His practical, sensible parents would
blush for their idiot son, Angus. He hugged Hillary
closely and said, "Shh. It'll be all right. Don't worry,
honey. We'll handle it."

The phone rang all day. There were calls from the
people Angus had searching in boats and boathouses
and from those taking seemingly casual trips on board
ships that were still in harbor, this long after Tate had
been taken. None had seen any sign of a strange female being where she had no business. He thanked
them all. And he made some calls. When he found
Hillary's big eyes watching him, he explained exactly
with whom he'd spoken. She began to relax.

Paul called. Robert MacLean had phoned him to
say the political boil was about to burst. It would be
in the morning papers, but it would be on television
that night. If this was what had caused Tate to be
snatched, she should be freed within hours.

Tate freed? Home? She'd see Tate!

Angus cautioned, "We don't know who took her.
This might not have anything to do with Tate."

"I just know it does. I just know she found out
something about one of the political underlings. Tate
will be free! See? We didn't *even* need Finnig!"

She ignored Angus's cautioning.

The excitement built. Angus tried to call Finnig and
had to leave a message, as usual, and they waited for
him to call back. Angus sent an agitated Hillary down
to swim, to work off some of the nervous energy that
was driving her to pacing and upsetting the cat. And
he volunteered that he wouldn't say anything to Paul
about Finnig's men—yet.

She swam for over an hour. Endless, countless laps. Then she stayed by the phone while Angus took a turn in the pool for another hour.

While Angus was swimming, Willie called. "It's coming. I can feel it."

"Oh, Willie, I'm *sure* this is it! The political thing. It's bursting tonight!"

And Willie's voice softened. "I'll come to you."

Hillary protested, "Oh, *no*! Uh, I don't think—"

But Willie had hung up.

When Angus came back from the pool, Hillary blurted pithily, "Willie's coming over."

His reaction was none at all. "Fine."

"What will we do when we have to leave? What will we say?"

"Honey, it's only four-thirty. We don't leave here until ten. That's five and a half hours. Willie isn't going to stay that long."

"I know that she's feeling very supportive. She feels this is a vigil. Willie's coming here to be sustaining through the crisis. She won't leave."

Angus kissed her and looked at her in a contemplating way. "You're fascinating." He patted her shoulder and went on to the shower.

With Willie not yet there, Hillary's brain was already scrambling around, trying to think of ways to get Willie to leave before they were to meet Finnig's men. Then Hillary thought that maybe Willie wouldn't come there after all. Or if she did, she'd only stay for a few minutes.

But, wearing her floating garments and a wide black straw hat, a laden Willie arrived to kiss their cheeks. She handed Angus a crock of some strange-looking, delicious-smelling concoction, and she directed him to

put it in the refrigerator. Willie then removed a bur-
geoningly active mass from a paper bag, washed her
hands, did a cupboard check for flour and wasn't
surprised there was none. She cleaned the cat ledge,
which also served as the kitchen counter. Then she
took a smaller bag from her linen sack purse, shook
flour out on the counter, added the dough and
punched down the awesome mass into something
manageable. After that she sought containers in which
to allow it to rise again before it was to be baked. She
did all this with an odd assortment of pans.

That completed, Willie washed her hands, removed her hat and smiled at Hillary. "All will be
well."

Hillary managed a smile. Willie would be there
through the dinner hour. How would they get rid of
her? "We have watermelon. Shall I make a fruit
salad?"

"Perfect." Willie bent down and picked up the cat,
who then confided in dulcet tones that she was being
neglected.

Willie *tsk*ed sympathetically, but she was chuck-
ling. She smiled at Angus and said, "The cat's name
is Phoebe."

Angus nodded. "She just told you that?"

"Yes. She told me she's being neglected and she's
very tired of being called 'Cat,' so she told me her
name is Phoebe."

Hillary accepted that, and Angus clapped two loud,
slow pops as he congratulated Willie, "You've got
yourself a cat!"

Willie demurred. "I didn't name her. I've only re-
lated to you what she told me."

"Yeah. Sure. What else did she tell you?"

"There were other men in Tate's apartment the night Finnig came here."

Angus frowned, and Hillary gasped.

"They listened to the phone tape," Willie translated.

Hillary accused, "Angus told you to say that!"

Willie looked up, surprised. "Why?"

"Because we were quarreling."

"Why?"

"I didn't want him to tell P—"

Willie's lashes fell over her eyes as she petted Phoebe. "He won't tell."

Hillary's tongue tangled. "What I mean is that I was saying, you see, I didn't want to impose on Angus, and he was saying— Were there really people in Tate's apartment that night, too?"

Phoebe made a single, lifting sound and stared at Hillary.

In some disgust that she was actually asking for a cat's verbal report, Hillary wouldn't quit. "Did... Phoebe really see some men in Tate's apartment?"

Willie's gray glance came up to Hillary and she said, "Phoebe told you, yes."

"Sure. What's her 'no' sound?"

And the cat gave a brief descending sound.

The hair on Angus and Hillary had to have stood out straight. How had the cat known to make another sound right at that time?

Angus said to Hillary, "See? If you hadn't been with me, you'd be wherever Tate is now. Just as I told you, that *would* have happened."

Hillary's eyes were wide, and she was holding herself stiffly. She asked Phoebe, "Did they go into the bedroom?"

The cat stared back and made the descending sound.

Hillary looked at Angus to mock his word, "*See?* I told you they wouldn't go into the bedroom."

"You listen to a cat?" he said, dismissing such foolishness.

Phoebe looked up at Willie and trilled a little series of sounds, and Willie laughed, although she did try to smother it.

Angus opened his mouth, but he stopped; he was damned if he would ask what a cat had said! So he asked Willie, "Is Paul coming for supper?"

"No."

"You two fight?"

"Nicely."

Willie sat cozily ensconced on the sofa with Phoebe, who was apparently telling her all the "family" secrets, like some six-year-old child, and Willie was encouraging it. The couple whose secrets they were did squirm and try for conversation. And Hillary kept checking her watch.

Jim came along in time for supper. Hillary knew he and Willie had planned it that way. They were supportive friends, and this was a night of crisis. There was more than enough food in Willie's crock, and the apartment was filled with the aroma of strangely shaped, freshly baked bread.

The table conversation was mostly between Willie and Jim. Hillary watched her watch, and Angus sat back, listening.

The news channel was on the television. So far there was nothing on the cable station about the political mess. Was the station being cautious? Or were they gathering material? Doing interviews? Finding some-one who would actually face a camera? Interesting. Would the mess blow up? Or would it blow out, in an ever-widening circle? Or did they still think it could be smoothed over? How? At what cost? Tate?

Hillary looked at her fingers, wondering, Who had Tate? Which of all those dramatic happenings had ensnared Tate? They should know tonight. It would be solved, Tate would be back in her life, and everything would go on as normal. That implied that turmoil was normal, for in all those normal days there had been something else going on that was so disruptive that it made the snatching of a woman plausible. How shocking were the workings of "ordinary" times.

So the time was approaching when Hillary and An-gus had to leave the apartment. One and then the other had gone discreetly into the bedroom to change into dark clothing. Hillary had on a dark blue turtleneck and trousers. Angus was in black.

Hillary's restlessness couldn't be ignored. Jim said, "What's going on?"

"Nothing!" Hillary bit her tongue. She'd replied too quickly.

"Never fool a fooler. What's up? Where are you going? With whom?"

Hillary shut up entirely. Angus fielded questions. He did a very good job of it, but he didn't lead Jim off the track. Jim drilled in, questioning, verbally shad-owboxing Angus. Willie watched, listening. Then she put Phoebe aside and went to the bathroom. When she returned to the living room, she picked up Phoebe and sat down. She said to Jim, "I think we should back off. Angus knows what he's doing. We'll stay and monitor the phone, okay?"

The two men paused, looked at Willie, then settled back and agreed. Angus snapped, "Did you talk to Paul?"

Serenely Willie replied, "No."

Hillary said, "It's time."

Jim asked Angus, "Why don't I go with Hillary? Whomever you're meeting won't know the difference between us. You be backup. I've had more experience with this sort of thing."

Angus rejected the help: "No." He *had* to be the one with Hillary. With his love.

Hillary was indignant. "How does he know we're meet—"

"I don't." Jim was standing restlessly. Laid-back, sleepy-eyed Jim was restless! Hillary marveled.

Jim continued. "I only know this night, of all nights, you should be here, and you're both impatient to get out of the apartment. You have to be meeting someone. Let me trail along."

"They'll quit." Angus got a raincoat from the coat closet. It was a light beige. Easily seen at night.

Angus's two friends watched that grimly. They knew Angus was making a target of himself. That was confirmed when he chose a dark raincoat for Hillary.

Very gravely, Jim said, "I see. Finnig's men."

"We have to go." Angus was regretful, but he shook Jim's hand, leaned to kiss Willie's cheek and put his hand on the small cat's head. "I don't know of better friends. Thanks anyway."

"You're tying our hands," Jim protested.

The only one who didn't say anything was Willie. And Phoebe.

As the two went down the exit hall, with Hillary almost running to keep up with Angus's long strides, she said, "Thank you for not telling them sooner. It's too late for them to call Paul and louse it up."

"This is a fool's setup."

"It'll be all right." She took his arm, her eyes pleading for understanding, for reassurance.

Being the woman she was, she'd always played trustingly by the rules. He knew that. If anything happened, he would see to it that she survived, but he couldn't have her live and not know that he loved her. She might not realize he was putting his life on the line for her only because he did love her, and he knew if he didn't go with her, she'd find a way to go alone. But she needed to know.

He stopped on the stair landing and pulled her to him. She was stopped midflight and was jarred against his hard chest. "Hillary." His eyes were very serious.

"What is it?"

"I love you."

"It's creeping up, isn't it." It wasn't a question; it was an admission.

"Look at me." Their stares locked. He wanted her to remember him. Like Jim and probably Willie, he had little faith that he would come out of this—unscathed. God only knew what sort of driven maniac they could be dealing with, and they had Finnig as their only buffer. While Finnig might look out for his own men, there was no commitment for him to watch out for two idiots. Angus had to see to it that Hillary survived no matter what kind of madness was going down. But if he didn't make it through this night, he wanted her to remember him.

Then he kissed her. It wasn't a harsh kiss; it was a yearning, lover's kiss. It told of all the hopes he'd had for them. The love and tenderness they could have shared. It shook him. And briefly, while he could be distracted, regret flooded his body.

The kiss confused Hillary. It wasn't the kind of quick, encouraging kiss she'd expected. It left her reeling with the emotion he'd conveyed to her. Not passion. Something beyond that to a meeting of souls. She grasped his body—and felt the shoulder holster. He was carrying a gun! That slim, deadly gun.

Hillary had been concentrated on Tate's release working out like in the films of her childhood. The rough street men would all have hearts of gold, and the captors would release Tate with good humor. It would all end up with Tate having had yet another of her adventures. Hillary had all that so firmly in her mind that she hadn't paid any attention to all the warnings Angus had tried to give to her. It was the yearning, lover's kiss that reached past her rose-colored world, but it was the gun that stunned her into reality. They were about to do something dangerous.

Hillary became calm and exceedingly alert.

Angus saw that as they looked at each other on the landing. After his kiss and before she felt the gun, he saw realization come into her eyes. Then he saw her rally. It might turn out all right after all. She was in control of herself. He said, "Good." And then he kissed her as she'd expected. A quick kiss of encouragement.

She smiled into his eyes, and they turned to go down the stairs—a team.

Ten

Angus and Hillary stood briefly at the apartment entrance, in the light, so that anyone watching would be able to identify them as two people who were waiting. Two people expecting to be contacted. Then they stood to the shadows, off to one side.

They stood quietly. The tension was so strong between them that it seemed anyone passing by would feel it, too. And finally two forms, similar in appearance, approached through the night.

Angus discreetly noted their approach and monitored it. Hillary stared at them the entire time. She saw that their heads swiveled as they watched the area without seeming to do it. Men did that anyway, she knew, but this was so perfectly done. It was interesting to see, to learn from watching it done so well.

Everything was under the two men's regard. Nothing moved that the two forms didn't note the move-

ment, assess it and register it. They came in the general
direction of the open entrance but not directly to the
waiting couple. When they finally did approach, it was
as if by happenstance.

One went on past and hesitated as if he hadn't
expected the other to stop. "Finnig," the first man
said. "Pretend you're giving me a match." He put a
cigarette into his mouth.

Angus felt in his pockets and then held out an empty
palm. The other man's hand barely touched Angus's,
but the man had a match concealed, lighted it and lit
his cigarette.

Angus questions, "Your names?"

"I'm Mark. He's Phillip. You?"

"Angus and Hillary." Angus wasn't sure how they
were supposed to identify themselves, but since it was
just first names for their contacts, he assumed that was
how he should do it, too. It appeared to satisfy Mark.

He said, "We'll go on ahead. There's a blue car,
'round the curve on the street, with a guy working on
the tire. He won't go with us. It's just so we can park
there. When we get to that tree, you two come along.
We'll get the car going, then you two get in the back
seat. Got it?"

"Yes," Angus replied.

Mark smiled a little. "Thanks for the match."

Angus relaxed a shade. "No trouble."

It seemed to take forever for Mark and Phillip to
pass the tree. Angus took Hillary's arm and gestured.
That was for any watcher. She thought the farce was
just a little silly. Who would watch? They followed as
they'd been instructed.

When they passed the curve there was a squad car,
and a policeman stood questioning the blue car being

parked at that place. Mark was smiling and gesturing a little in a coaxing way. Hillary slowed her steps, but Angus tugged her to keep up.

The cop was saying, "... towed."

"We'll help him," Mark replied. "He's a guy we know. A good man. Okay?"

The cop said, "Make it quick." Then he moved back toward his squad car, and he appeared to just see the couple approaching. He touched his hat and said, "G'evening."

Angus smiled. He recognized the man as one of Paul's, and he knew the policeman had the license number of the car. The cop returned to his car and drove away.

Mark said to the tire man, "We'll ride you a couple of blocks. Someone might be watching to see what you do."

"Okay."

Like magic the car was off the jack and the hood closed. Tools were put away, and the five got into the car. The three men sat in the front seat; Angus and Hillary were in the back. After a couple of blocks, at a traffic light, the extra man exited the car and vanished into the evening crowd.

The car turned south into the city and eventually went east. They drove for a long time. The car radio was on; the music finished and a news brief said the chairman of the board had resigned from Will-Kel, Inc.

Angus and Hillary exchanged a questioning look. Was that important to Tate?

It was then that Mark reached over and changed the station. There was no talking in the car. They simply drove on eastward. They went through city streets instead of taking the thruways.

The neighborhoods changed. Once-great houses and fine homes had been trashed and barricaded. There was antique litter, and chain links over the stores' windows. Hillary reached over and locked the car door. So did Angus. But making Hillary's spine really shiver, so did Mark and Phillip lock their doors.

They continued to drive, and the traffic thinned. Then they came to an obsolete industrial section. The car slowed. It was dark. Big, dirty buildings loomed. The streetlights were inadequate. There was no traffic, no pedestrians. It was spooky.

Hillary had just thought, Surely, not here, when Mark said, "We're almost there."

"You're not going to leave us here," she gasped.

"Naw, course not." Phillip spoke for the first time.

Mark said, "There's a car in back of us."

Phillip slowed the car to a crawl. Hillary turned around to look, saw a car hesitate as if reluctant to pass them. Then it stopped, backed and turned into another street.

"You guys tell anybody?" Mark was looking back over his shoulder at them.

Angus said, "No."

Phillip accused, "There's been differen' cars the whole way."

Angus soothed, "These are public streets. Cars on them can't be unusual."

"All behind us," Phillip groused. "Nobody passed us."

Angus said, "Settle down. You're not wanted for anything. This is a legit cause. You're the good guys."

"I don't need no cops," Phillip declared again. He gunned the motor, squealed around a corner and stopped. "Out," he commanded.

Angus protested, "Not here. Not Hillary."

Hillary objected, "We didn't tell anyone. You're making a mistake."

"Out." Mark turned, and a gun bore was peeking over his arm.

For Hillary it was ludicrous.

Angus said, "Tell Finnig thanks a whole lot. And you explain exactly where you left us. Understand? He's going to nail your hides to the wall."

Phillip argued, "He told ya no cops."

"You explain exactly where you left us," Angus insisted again. Apparently they had a greater fear of cops than they had of Finnig.

Hillary was so indignant that she said, "Let's go. It's their skins."

The two reject passengers got out of the car and it took off, leaving them there in the total silence. They looked around. With all the people in Chicago, how did this pocket of silence exist?

They both wore running shoes. Angus took off his raincoat and turned it inside out. It was dark on the new side. Had he worn its light side in that dark place, it could only have attracted attention to them—to Hillary. Now Angus wanted them to be as invisible as possible. He put the coat back on and they established their bearings.

Quietly Angus said, "Since they were coming down that street, we'll go back to it and continue on down it. It eventually reaches the lake. We'll see if we can still salvage this. Don't get away from me. Stick close to me. Do exactly as I say. No matter what happens."

"Yes."

"I mean exactly that." His voice was stern.

"So do I."

When they came to the corner, Angus looked for the other car, but none was anywhere around. It probably hadn't been cops. Damn. What were Mark and Phillip involved in that cops would make them so nervous that they'd risk Finnig's wrath? Finnig would be furious! Maybe.

They began to walk. It was another world. Their steps were silent, the night was silent, the dark streets were silent. They walked through a vacuum.

Hillary whispered, "We had a whistle signal as children."

The two stopped and looked at each other. Should they risk calling attention to themselves? But if Tate was in any of these buildings, they could walk right on past. Angus asked, "How loud can you whistle?"

She replied, "Stand back."

Her eyes were used to the dark, and she saw that he smiled at her. He encouraged, "Blast away."

She licked her lips, braced herself, took a deep breath and put two fingers in her mouth to shatter the night air with two upper tones and a downer.

Angus was impressed. They listened. Nothing.

He knew that in that atmosphere the whistle would be heard for blocks. Whose ears would get the signal? A gang thinking their rivals were issuing a challenge? What were they risking, these two people so out of their own element? At least, Hillary was. Alone, he could handle anything. It was his responsibility to Hillary that was the stick in the spokes of the wheel.

Again Hillary took a deep breath, and this time Angus joined perfectly in the whistle, which should have jarred all the wax out of any ears within a six-block radius. He didn't need to use his fingers.

They heard a whistling reply. One sharp blast. Angus grinned. But Hillary shook her head. "That's not the reply."

They began to walk again, farther from the center of town. In the dark, deserted street. Alone.

Then they heard it. Not too close. An upper note and one lower. The real reply. But from where?

It took them a while. They ran to a corner and whistled, then listened. They went the wrong way several times and had to backtrack. The buildings absorbed and deflected the sounds. It took time.

But they came finally to a cross street, and the whistle was from the left. They approached openly. If Tate was whistling, no one else must be there or they would stop her.

They were almost down the street when they heard running steps coming toward them. Gangs? Then the whistle reply came from the building across the street. Hillary didn't risk whistling back. Angus took her arm, and they crossed the street and ran along the building to the corner. The sound of steps had stopped. Where?

They both wondered if someone was interfering with the signals. Like kids replying to someone else's mother when she called her kids to come home.

Angus had drawn his gun, they went around the corner and a car approached. Who? There was a cul-de-sac at the entrance into the building, and they ducked inside. Angus pulled Hillary between himself and the building. The car stopped just beyond the entrance and out of sight. There were voices, then it drove on. Angus peeked out and the street was de-

serted. They tried the door, and it opened into shad-
owy gloom, with dark masses of... machinery? Just
as Willie's friend had predicted.

Hillary yelled, "Tate!"

"I'm here, Boy."

"Any problems?"

"No. They're all gone. Come on up."

"How?"

"There's a stair to your left."

Angus, of course, had a pocket flashlight; they
found a long metal staircase and went up carefully,
Angus going first, both looking around. Why wasn't
Tate coming to them?

When they got to the top of the stairs, they saw a slit
of light.

"Tate?" Hillary called again.

"I'm here. What are you doing in town? The ten
days aren't up yet."

Angus questioned, "Anyone there with you?"

"Just Carter. The others left a while ago."

They went to the cloth-covered doorway. Angus
pushed Hillary against the wall, and he had the gun
ready as he ripped the cloth aside.

Nothing happened.

Tate said, "Smart. But it's really okay."

He peeked. Nothing. He shot a look at Hillary and
whispered, "Don't move." He leaped across the
opening and whirled to crouch and look again. Then
he stood and carefully looked. He said, "Hello, Tate.
We finally meet. Are they really all gone? Who were
they?"

"I honestly have no idea who actually snatched us.
I've almost got this blasted knot undone—" Then she
saw Hillary. "Oh, darling, how nice to see you. Why

are you here? I couldn't believe the whistle. You remembered that? How marvelous!''

Hillary hugged her sister tightly, and their smiles were watery. "I'd already dieted," Hillary complained. "I didn't need to lose any more weight worrying about you."

"Where did you find him?" Tate's eyes sparkled as she looked at Angus. And she indicated the soft rope knot on her wrists for Hillary's fingers to open.

"It's a long story." Hillary worked the knot free.

Angus had freed the other woman. "Carter, I presume? We've hunted for you all over Chicago."

Verna Carter was thirty years old, a very light blonde with dark brown eyes who had a great smile. "You've missed an interesting time. Hello, Hillary."

"I thought you were a man."

"I don't *think* so." Carter frowned as she considered the new idea.

Tate laughed and Angus grinned. When Hillary finally could, she asked, "Why were you taken?"

"Apparently it began at lunch one day. I was alone in a niche at Fiona's, and I overheard a conversation among some Young Turks.... Do you know the expression 'Beware the Young Turks' goes back over two thousand years? Think how strong that must have been to survive this long. Like 'Beware of Greeks bearing gifts.'''

"Tate." Hillary gave her a patient reminder to stick to the subject.

"I was editing an article while I ate lunch, behind the palms in that one corner, and really, I wasn't paying that much attention. But when I left, I did note the table of, oh, five or six men who were appalled to see me suddenly appear. So much so that I glanced back as I left, and I saw one urgently ask Fiona about me. I knew he wasn't attracted to me, but he pulled her over in order for her to ID me. I racked my brain and recalled something they'd said about a fight to remove the old guard. There was a scandal brewing. It was a fight for change. Something made me uneasy. Something in the manner of the man who questioned Fiona—"

"A hunch," Hillary guessed.

"Right. So I set the clues and wrote you the note. It was the next day that they took us, but it was with great courtesy and consideration."

"You were brilliant," Hillary told her sister.

"So were you. You came after me."

Hillary declined the credit. "It was Angus and his friends."

Chewing on the unsolved puzzle, Angus said, "It could have been the political group." But then he shook his head as he mentioned, "The chairman resigned from Will-Kel, Inc. today."

Tate smiled. "I wonder if they were the ones."

Hillary looked at Angus. "Which was it?"

He slowly shook his head a couple of times and shrugged.

Tate asked, "What else did you think it was?"

"Angus has a cop friend, Paul, who found several things that it could have been, but telling about all that can wait until we get you back home."

Angus had to ask again, "You really don't know who snatched you? Who kept you here?"

"We have no idea. They wore partial masks. With bulges over their cheekbones and chins. They wore caps and golf gloves and identical gray jumpsuits. They were as nice as they could be. We played a whole lot of poker. They rarely spoke, and then it was only in whispers. But—and this is interesting—they knew someone was looking for us who has clout and contacts. They were very nervous about it. I heard some whispers. They could be a little careless. Once this day was past, it didn't matter who knew what. They simply needed time. But whoever the power was who was looking for us stimulated them. It was like a game to them."

Angus and Hillary exchanged a surprised look. "Paul wouldn't carry that kind of clout."

Then they both questioned at the same time, "Finnig?"

"Who's Finnig?" Tate asked. "How did you find us?"

Angus put off replying. "Right now what we have to do is get you out of here. Did they just leave you here to rot?"

"No. They did tie us, but it was calculated so that we could get loose, and they said they'd let the authorities know where we were. But they've only been gone about a half hour. At best our rescuers won't be here for another hour. It will be interesting to see who turns up."

Carter complained, "I've only known Tate for six months, and this is the second time I've been missing. The last time was when I went after that damned fish and took a wrong turn."

Hillary was no comfort. "You ought to have grown up in the same house with her. She was always stirring things up. I'm glad you remembered the whistle, Tate. With you tied up that way, it's a good thing you didn't need your fingers to whistle. Why did you only whistle that once?"

"That wasn't I."

Hillary and Angus looked at each other yet again. The footsteps on the street? What if those people hadn't left with the car? If they didn't get in the car, where did they go? Were they in the building? Angus went out the door silently. And in about ten seconds came back inside . . . with Paul.

Hillary looked at Paul, then her cold eyes moved to Angus. So he *had* called Paul, who had followed them. Finnig's men had been right.

Angus said, "Ladies, I've found you a way home."

Tate and Carter were a little stimulated with their rescue, so, with Paul, they all went to Tate's apartment. Along the way they collected the two who still waited at Angus's place: Jim and Willie, who carried Phoebe. It was close to two a.m.

They drank a toast to liberation. And a bouquet of flowers arrived. To Tate. "Welcome home again" was typed on the card. Who? Paul went downstairs and returned to say, "A man in a gray jumpsuit. With a scarlet baseball cap."

Tate smiled at the flowers. "They all had class."

Of course, Paul tried to trace the flowers, and there wasn't any way at all. The bouquet was a beautiful mixture of many kinds of flowers. Paul explained, "They could have bought a single kind at several places and combined them. In order to do that, they had to buy them the day before, during business hours."

Tate said with some satisfaction, "How cheeky of them."

Jim mentioned, "That's exactly the kind of reckless thing that gets people caught."

Carter countered, "I hope not."

Everyone looked at her, and Tate laughed out loud.

Willie's eyes almost closed, and she said something to the cat, whose reply was a down note.

Among those in Tate's apartment that night, it was avidly debated how and with whom the snatchers had been involved.

"Whoever they were, they were the good guys." Tate was sure.

"They held you against your will," Paul reminded her. "They committed a criminal act. We'll look for them."

Tate reminded Paul, "No harm was done."

"You're not going to file charges?"

"On whom?" she inquired.

"Damn." Paul was even holding the pad and pencil, which probably prevented Tate's ears from being singed.

As the wine was passed and everyone talked over everyone else and questions were answered, Angus gradually realized that not only was Hillary ignoring him; she was *furious* with him! He tried to figure out why.

So he cornered her in the kitchen and asked, "Have you decided I've served my purpose and you can snub me now?"

"You phoned Paul! I *forbade* you to, but you went right ahead and called him, just the way you did that first morning."

"I did nothing of the sort."

"You told me you called him that first morning."

Angus admitted, "Then I did, but—"

"See? And you did it again today when I specifically *forbade* your doing it and putting Tate in danger."

"Apparently she was never *in* any danger," he reminded her.

"You didn't know that."

"I did not phone Paul."

It was one of those arguments that never really got past the accusatory stage and just made the participants angrier.

A little after three a.m., Angus said good-night, his eyes on Hillary, but she ignored him. Very disgruntled, he picked up his cat and went home. He figured Hillary probably would sleep at Tate's. He unlocked his door, went inside, put the cat down and closed the door.

At Tate's, Willie followed Hillary into the kitchen and asked, "Why are you and Angus quarreling?"

"How did you know?"

Pointedly, Willie looked at Hillary's tight lips and tear-filmed eyes, expecting Hillary to at least smile as she said, "I'm psychic."

"Oh. That's right." Her eyes puddled. "Angus betrayed my trust."

"How?"

If Willie was psychic, why was she asking? "He phoned Paul."

"So? They're friends."

"He told Paul where we were going tonight."

"No. Angus didn't tell Paul. I did."

"You? How did you know? Did you 'see' it?"

"No. I only warned him something was up. When I called you, you tried to stop me from coming over. I knew tonight was the crux of the whole thing, and I couldn't understand why you wouldn't want me here. So I called Paul. He had the apartment complex watched."

"And Angus—?"

"He had no clue. I phoned Paul," Willie promised.

"Oh." Hillary was forlorn. "I've been hateful to Angus."

"And he's done everything he could to help you."

Hillary suggested, "I'd better go and apologize."

"That would be nice." Willie wondered if Paul appreciated how mature she was in comparison to Hillary.

Hillary went to Tate. "I'll see you in the morning."

"You don't have to go to a hotel, honey. That bed's big enough for both of us."

"I'll be in apartment nine. The number is a six, but it's really a nine."

Tate squinted as she sorted it out.

Hillary sighed. "It's a long, involved story, and I'll tell it all to you tomorrow. I'm so glad you're okay. I really had some quivers of worry."

They hugged each other fondly. Tate was serious as she said, "If there'd been danger, I wouldn't have involved you."

"How could you possibly know you were safe?" Hillary asked.

"They only needed time."

"I suppose we'll have the opportunity to sort all this out before I go back to Kansas City?"

"That will depend on you. This Angus is a gorgeous man. You're going to him?"

"There's been a misunderstanding. When I tell you everything, you'll see how it was."

"I can hardly wait. Good night, little sister. I love you. Thank you for coming to my rescue. Someday—" Tate stopped.

"Someday I'll find Benjamin."

Tate's sad eyes closed. "Yes."

"I will. Nothing will stop my hunting."

With her promise, Hillary said good-night, took up her coat and left. She went down the hall to Angus's apartment.

Angus had undressed and put on his pajama bottoms. With the lights out, he went into the kitchen and made himself a drink. He stood in the dark apartment, staring out the windows, over the city lights, and turned to look out over the water. It should have been a peaceful scene.

How could she have accused him of betraying her? He'd bent over backward to do everything her way. Risked their very lives! And she was mad at him. She wouldn't even give him the chance to defend himself. What a mess. Damn.

He was still grinding his teeth when he heard someone touch his hall doorknob. He put his glass down on a towel on the kitchen counter so that its sound was deadened. Then he slipped silently into the bedroom to pull his gun from its holster. Carefully, he returned to the kitchen as he heard someone working on his lock. Finnig? Or was it a battered Mark and Phillip?

He raised the gun as the lock clicked and the door opened. It was a short silhouette. He lowered the gun to the figure's new height, and then he saw that it was . . . Hillary. Phoebe greeted her like a good hostess, and Hillary replied. The cat followed Hillary as she went into the bedroom—having walked past the kitchen door, where Angus stood in the dark.

His mind darted around into a remarkably fast evaluation: she was there! She could be angry with him and still come to share his bed? She wasn't a woman who shunned a man until he crawled? He was riveted. His hands gradually lowered the gun. And he stood there in a haze of love for her.

But maybe she'd just come to gather her things and move out.

By moving just a little, he could look into the living-room mirror and see her as she moved about in a portion of the bedroom. Then she went into the bathroom and shut the door.

If she'd gone in there to gather her things, she wouldn't have shut the door, would she? Then he heard the shower! Tate had a shower; Hillary didn't need to shower here—unless she was getting ready for bed.

Like lightning, he reset the safety on the gun and rushed to put it back into its holster. He ripped off his pajama bottoms and then had to straighten them so he could hang them on the back of the door. He grabbed clean underwear from his drawer and took up the dark trousers and pullover he'd worn that night. He darted back into the kitchen and began to dress. At the last minute he ran for his shoes, but the shower was turned off and he couldn't get socks.

He ran back to the darkened kitchen, breathing through his mouth to soften the sound. He pushed his feet into his shoes. His ears were tuned to the bedroom. *She was getting into his bed.*

He waited. Brilliantly, he waited, very proud of his self-control. Then he slipped out of his shoes, and, carrying them, he went to the hall door. He inserted his key and carefully made the natural noises. Back in his shoes, he opened and closed the door. Would she call out? Come to him?

That darling Phoebe came to greet him. Actually she came to see what the hell he was doing, he knew. But either way, he could speak to her. In a tired, discouraged voice. The voice of a scorned man. He wondered if Hillary could catch the nuances. His sigh, which ought to wring her heartless heart.

He went into the kitchen and opened the cupboard, closed it and picked up the glass from the counter. He opened the freezer and rattled the ice cubes, then pulled the cork from the wine bottle he'd left on the sink before he poured more seltzer into the rest of his drink. He rattled the ice in the glass and went to stand in the window.

He smiled because he was making her wait.

She deserved it for not trusting him. For condemning him without a trial. An honest man. But she'd come to him. She wasn't pulling any female histrionics on him. She was willing to listen after all. She deserved to be let off the hook.

He put the glass in the sink with a thump, ran some water to cover the sound of his pouring out the rest of the mix, and strolled into the bedroom. He scanned the bed from the corners of his eyes. There she was. On her side of the center line.

He took off his pullover and trousers and hung them away, his back to her, and he sighed again.

There was a giggle from the bed!

He whipped around and glared. She was laughing at him? He stopped and feigned surprise. "Goldilocks!"

She smiled gently. "Come on, Behr, you knew I was here."

"How?"

"I saw you in the mirror and you were in your pajamas."

"Damn. I've just done a brilliant job of it, and it was all wasted. Why didn't you say something?"

"I wanted to see what you'd do."

"So you let me make a fool of myself."

"You're precious to me." This vulnerable, imaginative, brave man, she thought.

"I wasn't earlier."

"Forgive me. I'll never again doubt you. You were magnificent tonight.... You have been since I first met you. You're a true man. I don't know what I would have done without you. Thank you."

"You're welcome." And at last he acknowledged that Hillary was maybe a bit more mature than he—in some ways.

More leisurely, not quite certain yet, he finished undressing, but he didn't take the pajamas from the door. He went to the bed, lifted the sheet and crawled over to the center line. "Somebody's been sleeping in my bed, and there she is!"

She had the sheet up to her chin, and she was watching him.

He tried again. "You're here."

"Yes."

"Is it time for love? Or are we still working on friendship?"

"I believe the love has been here almost from the beginning. I've never in my life seen such green eyes."

"Does that balance the snake-mark problem?"

"Well, I did feel I shouldn't leave the applications only halfway done. A promise of help is a firm commitment. I was obligated to return and keep my word."

"I like a dedicated woman."

"You haven't forgotten my mosquito bites?" She lowered the top of the sheet to reveal that the problem still existed.

He took a quick, excited breath. "Not for a minute."

"Never? Even when Mark and Phillip put us out on that deserted, spooky street?"

"You were mine. I needed to watch out for you. That included the mosquito bites."

"Angus, are you free and clear? Can I become involved with you?"

"You have no choice. You are involved."

"And you?" she asked.

"Me, too."

"I believe I really love you, but I am committed to finding Benjamin, and I need a little time to be sure my feelings for you aren't caused by meeting a very clever city slicker. One who changes his door number to trap unsuspecting newcomers."

"Well, one does as one must."

"We have to get the number fixed so that no other female wanders in."

"Right now?"

"In the morning will do just fine."

"I'd be perfectly willing to get up and go hammer in a nail right now."

"Never mind. I'd rather you come over here."

He moved across the center line. "You got something that needs hammering?"

"It's these damned mosquito bites."

He drew a deep, patient breath. "A man's work is never done."

* * * * *

*Read Tate's story in Silhouette Desire #453,
HIDE AND SEEK, which is coming out in
October 1988. Be sure to find it!*

Silhouette Romance

LONG, TALL TEXANS

A Trilogy by Diana Palmer

Bestselling Diana Palmer has rustled up three rugged heroes in a trilogy sure to lasso your heart! The titles of the books are your introduction to these unforgettable men:

CALHOUN

In June, meet Calhoun Ballenger. He wants to protect Abby Clark from the world, but can he protect her from himself?

JUSTIN

Calhoun's brother, Justin—the strong, silent type—has a second chance with the woman of his dreams, Shelby Jacobs, in August.

TYLER

October's long, tall Texan is Shelby's virile brother, Tyler, who teaches shy Nell Regan to trust her instincts—especially when they lead her into his arms!

Don't miss CALHOUN, JUSTIN and TYLER—three gripping new stories coming soon from Silhouette Romance!

Silhouette Desire

COMING NEXT MONTH

#439 THE CASTLE KEEP—Jennifer Greene
Although architect Micheal Fitzgerald had made a career out of building walls, he'd never seen defenses like Carra O'Neill's—defenses he planned on breaking down with a little Irish magic.

#440 OUT OF THE COLD—Robin Elliott
When Joshua Quinn was sent to protect Kristin Duquesne, he wasn't supposed to fall in love with her. But he had . . . and now both their lives were in danger.

#441 RELUCTANT PARTNERS—Judith McWilliams
Elspeth Fielding had her own reasons for agreeing to live in a rustic cabin with James Murdoch. But after she met the reclusive novelist, the only important reason was him!

#442 HEAVEN SENT—Erica Spindler
A fulfilling career was Jessica Mann's idea of "having it all"—until she met Clay Jones and fulfillment took on a very different meaning.

#443 A FRIEND IN NEED—Cathie Linz
When Kyle O'Reilly—her unrequited college crush—returned unexpectedly, Victoria Winters panicked. She *refused* to succumb to her continuing attraction, but she could hardly kick him out—it was his apartment.

#444 REACH FOR THE MOON—Joyce Thies
The second of three *Tales of the Rising Moon*. Samantha Charles didn't accept charity, especially from the high and mighty Steven Armstrong, but a twist of fate had her accepting far more!

AVAILABLE NOW:

Silhouette Intimate Moments

At Dodd Memorial Hospital, Love is the Best Medicine

When temperatures are rising and pulses are racing, Dodd Memorial Hospital is the place to be. Every doctor, nurse and patient is a heart specialist, and their favorite prescription is a little romance. This month, finish Lucy Hamilton's Dodd Memorial Hospital Trilogy with HEARTBEATS, IM #245.

Nurse Vanessa Rice thought police sergeant Clay Williams was the most annoying man she knew. Then he showed up at Dodd Memorial with a gunshot wound, and the least she could do was be friends with him—if he'd let her. But Clay was interested in something more, and Vanessa didn't want that kind of commitment. She had a career that was important to her, and there was no room in her life for any man. But Clay was determined to show her that they could have a future together—and that there are times when the patient knows best.
